MURDER AND CONSPIRACY

AUTHOR

NIDHI GUPTA

"SARKAR"

Publisher: Self Publishing the book

ISBN: 978-93-5526-004-8

THANK YOU!

Creating anything in the world, has never been an easy task.
I sincerely thank God, who gave me the inspiration and energy to write this book.
And to the parents, who gave their blessings in accomplishing this.
Chiggu, my dear son, whose smiles and naughtiness inspire and refresh me.

DISCLAIMER

The stories mentioned in this book are inspired by contemporary events of the present period, but these stories are work of fiction completely, and should be read as fiction only. They are not related with any real event, person, country, place, living or dead, past or present or future. If it is found to be similar to any real event, person, country, place, then it will be a coincidence only.

Further, the names, events, places in this book are fictionally chosen for those stories. Its purpose is not to hurt any person, religion, caste, country and their citizens.

AUTHOR INTRODUCTION

Nidhi Gupta "Sarkar" is a writer of versatility. While she has run her pen on many prose genres like novel, story, essay etc., she has also written many poems.

She did her graduation in English Literature. But she has command in both languages, Hindi and English. To reaches masses, she uses both languages for her writing. She believed that it is easier to express one's thoughts in the mother tongue.

In her works, she has written on subjects like art, philosophy, psychology, society, nation, humanity etc.

Language and writing style of Nidhi Gupta:

There are two forms of the language of Nidhi Gupta "Sarkar" - the language is simple and easy to understand, in an intelligible form. But at some places the language becomes classical, while the words of the language have been selected prominently according to the character and place of the story.

Talking about the style, it keeps changing according to the theme. Sometimes it becomes descriptive, sometimes it becomes reflective.

Her stories are not limited to any particular country or place, in her stories, she sometimes take the reader to Kashmir in India, and sometimes China or Iraq. She has written those stories by portraying different people from all over the world. In addition, the impact of contemporary events is also reflected.

The issues of women are clearly visible in her stories. Whether it is China's Uyghur community or the Iraq War, women have suffered instability and the effects of war. (Story: Daughter of Iraq and In the Clutches of the Dragon). The continuing terrorism in Kashmir also had a negative impact on the women there, which was a subject of the author's stories. (Story: To Regret). Apart from this, women also have to bear the brunt of domestic violence and sexual abuse, whether it is from the husband or the father (story: Murder of the Father)

If a woman wants to achieve a position in society by making a goal for her, she has to surrender to the wrong desires of the people, which ultimately lead to degradation and exploitation (Story: Gangster Wife).

Even, if she refuses to bow down to them, she has to bear the fire of other's ego, jealousy and fire of revenge. (Story: Revenge of Love, Those closeness).

But in every case, despite suffering, the struggle and protest against oppression and tyranny is depicted.

She has chosen the words in her stories very carefully. And used very clean words. Because of this, not only the stories can be read for healthy entertainment, but it can also be learnt how to make the story interesting without using any vulgar words, and also without abusing.

SUMMARY

1. DAUGHTER OF IRAQ

This is the story of a brave woman living in Iraq, whose village is attacked and the terrorists kidnap her and all the people of her village. And then terrorists take her to their camp. Her days were passing while suffering atrocities in the camp.

Will she be able to meet her husband and son while coping with all this? Will she be able to rescue all her people from the clutches of terrorists?

2. IN THE CLUTCHES OF THE DRAGON

It tells about the atrocities on Uyghur Muslims of China. A Uyghur woman is abducted and subjected to horrific torture. Then some scientific experiments are done on her. What kind of research those scientists were doing? Then how does that woman escape from all this?

At the same time, the story of a Chinese scientist also runs side by side. He tests on bacteria and viruses. But what happens, that his own daughter becomes a victim of an unknown disease and that scientist is also forced to die.

3. AN ENTANGLED MURDER CASE

A nun gets murdered. Then the corpse is thrown into the well. The policemen who investigate the case, are bought. The policemen who unable to be purchased, are forced to commit suicide or removed out of the way.

Then the media and the courts intervene. There was an important evidence of this case - a CD. When it reaches the court, there is nothing special in it. Perhaps, the criminals have already changed it. Can the original CD come out?

Then how are those criminals be punished? Or do they succeed in suppressing the case with the help of their own money and power?

Who was behind all this? And what was the reason for the murder? Did the deceased have any important information that led to her murder?

4.   GANGSTER WIFE

This is the story of Vinita, a girl who comes to Washington City with her dreams. She makes every compromise for her success, but everywhere, she is exploited. In the glare of success, her life turns in the wrong direction. She gets murdered. Who killed her? Whether her husband, who was thinking of getting divorced with her? Or one of the people, whom she was blackmailing?

5.   TO REGRET

In this story, an innocent child named Ahmed is picked up by the terrorists. Then, he grows up to be a ruthless terrorist. Then years later, he is sent to terrorize the Kashmir. One night he and his companions hide in a house, and kill the whole family. But suddenly, Ahmed comes to know such a thing that he starts to regret about murder committed there.

6.   THOSE CLOSENESS

Both Daksh and Varsha, although being married to someone else, became close with each other. Just then the bell rings and Varsha shocked to see a man at the door. Who was that person?

Daksh suddenly goes missing, and then news comes of his death. Who killed him? Was Varsha had her hand in all this or of the person who had secretly come to her house that night?

7. REVENGE OF LOVE

Nirmala's husband gets kidnapped. She informs this to the police. Then it comes out that the strings of her husband's kidnapping are related with her past life. About ten years ago, when Nirmala was in her raw age. What happened at that time? Did Nirmala do any mistake? Or was someone taking revenge on her? Who was behind her husband's kidnapping? Could the police be able find her husband or not?

8. MURDER OF THE FATHER

Three girls, after the death of their mother, have to face the atrocities of their father. Why their father was torturing them? What was in his mind?

Then something happens that, all the three girls kill their own father, but the reason for the murder was, not the atrocities being committed on the girls by their father.

Then, why did those girls kill their father? What was the reason for this?

Who was behind all this? Could the offender get punished?

9.   TWO FOREIGN SPIES

The story is about two foreign spies who take advantage of the chaos in the government system and the interference of politicians. Taking advantage of the stupidity and sentiments of the public, they collect money. Then they make a plan to cause riots in the city by blowing up a temple with a bomb. One day in that temple, a guard is killed and thereafter riots broke out in the city. Then whether they are caught? or succeed in their plan?

CONTENTS

CHAPTER 1
DAUGHTER OF IRAQ

Abu Ishaq was lived in a village in northern Iraq. He had a shop of cashew, dates and nuts in a narrow street there. In that area, a very good crop of dates were grown. Good quality stock was available at reasonable rates. It was a work of honesty and efforts. He earned enough money. He had an ancestral house in which he lived with his mother, father and the family of his uncle. The house was old, but it was well built. There was a well inside, which gave very cold water. He had planted shady trees and plants in the courtyard.

One evening, Abu was returning home from his shop. That day, his business had gone very good. At that very moment, he found a dog in the street. Seeing Abu, he started barking not knowing why. Seeing his actions, Abu understood that perhaps the dog was mad, and was in the course of biting him. He turned to the other side. But the dog made him run. Abu ran away in fear. Dog chased behind him. While running, he entered another street, which was closed from the other side. Where could he go now? The dog came running and bit Abu in the left leg. There was a deep wound. Abu groaned in pain. There was a lot of bleeding.

Somehow he tied his handkerchief to the wound and came home limping. Seeing blood oozing from his leg, his mother and father got terrified. His mother put her hands on her ears and said-

—"Oh God! What happened to your feet?"

His father supported him and made him sit on the cot.
Abu told-

—"There was a dog in the back street, he made me ran and bit me."

His mother came with a box of first aid. His father cleaned the wound, then put ointment on it and bandaged it.
In no time Abu's uncle also came. He looked at the wound carefully.

Then advised-
—"I think the dog must have been mad. We should not believe these street dogs. If you agree with me, go to the health center and get the injection."

Abu said-
—"Okay uncle, I will go there just tomorrow."

Uncle said again-
—"Get ready in the morning. I'll take you there on my bike."

The next day Abu, accompanied by his uncle, went to the government hospital there. It was a government hospital with walls painted in yellow colour, which provided treatment at nominal cost. On entering, there was a verandah, where chairs were lying. There was a reception at one corner, where appointments were made. Thereafter, there were the doctors' rooms etc. At the hospital, he met compounder at the reception. He spoke-
—"I have to get an appointment for the treatment."

The compounder started making slip-
—"Name?"

—"Abu Ishaq."

—"Age?"

—"Twenty-three years."

—"What happened to you?"

—"I was bitten by the dog in the left leg."

—" Take this slip, sit there and wait for your turn. We are calling you after a while."

After getting the slip in the hospital, Abu sat there on a chair in the hallway of the hospital and waited for his turn.
After a while a nurse called out-
—"Who is Abu Ishaq, Abu Ishaq......?"

Abu stood up. Spoke-
—"Yes, I am."

The nurse said-
—"Come here. Your turn has come."

He reached to the dressing table. The doctor checked the wound by opening the bandage. The doctor said-
—"It's a very deep wound. But the first aid you did at home, did well. Well, I'll change the bandage."

Abu said-
—"Okay, sir."

Then the doctor applied ointment to the wound and tied a new bandage. Then on the prescription, he wrote 6 doses of injection for dog bite and sent him to the nurse outside-
—"The wound will heal well. You have to take six injections for the dog bite. Along with injections, keep getting changed the bandage every alternate day."

Abu came out and met the nurse. The nurse's name was Zarina. There was a white iron bed in the room, on which a beige colored bedsheet was spread. The nurse put laid down Ishaq on the bed and started preparing the injection. Ishaq rolled up his sleeve. After preparing the injection, the nurse brought the injection to the bed, placing it in a tray. When she saw Abu folded his sleeves, she was surprised. She said-
—"Hey, injection for dog bite is always given in the stomach, don't you know? Lie down on the bed. And pull your shirt off your stomach."

Ishaq lied down on the bed he put his shirt off his stomach. He was already frightened by the injection, he got even more nervous by hearing that the injection will go in the stomach. Zarina was efficient. She injected in the stomach and asked the name to work out the patient's nervousness and divide his attention-
—"I'm called Zarina and your name....?"

Ishaq told his name. But the injection was very painful and Ishaq's scream came out, but seeing the woman in front, he hid his pain.

The next day again, Abu reached the hospital to get the injection.
It was a Saturday, so everyone in the hospital was wearing casual clothes. Zarina was wearing a long traditional white gown, which had embroidery on both sides. She was looking very beautiful. There was no dress for a nurse in that hospital. Only a blue coat had to be worn over clothes that day. She wore a scarf to cover her head.
Zarina injected Abu. That day, Abu was no longer nervous, and his pain also subsided.

After the injection, Abu take his hand in his bag. He had brought some packets of dates as gift to the nurse. He extended the packet towards Zarina and said-
—"This is for you."

The nurse asked in surprise-
—"What is this?"

Abu told-
—"We have a business of dates and nuts, I have brought this for you."

Zarina refused-
—"Thanks, but I can't take it."
On very much insistence, Zarina agreed to get the dates.

In the course of six injections, Zarina and Ishaq became well acquainted. While Abu was enamored of Zarina's beauty, Zarina also started liking Abu because of his good manners, behavior and politeness of conversation. Then, After being recovered, Abu sent his uncle to Zarina's parents for relationship proposal. Abu used to earn well. His parents were from a reputed family. Zarina, on the other hand, was a skilled nurse, and apart from beauty, she was also adept in household chores. So both the parties agreed. Both sent clothes and sweets, nuts etc. to each other's house in goodfaith.

The Qazi of the city picked out the day of marriage. That day Abu reached Zarina's house with a marriage-party. He was wearing a sehra of beautiful red and white flowers, and was riding on a camel. The procession received a grand welcome at Zarina's house. Zarina was in the curtains with the women of her house.
Qazi asked -
—"Do you accept marriage?"

Zarina said shyly-
—"I accept."

This was repeated three times. Then the Qazi asked Abu.
After his acceptance, both sides congratulated each other. A lot of food and drink was offered to guests thereafter. On the second day, Zarina was given farewell by her parents. At the time of farewell, they gave her many gifts and household items.

After the marriage, both of them started living a happy life. Ishaq enhanced his business and started exporting dates abroad. Zarina, after her returning from the hospital, she looked after the household chores, serving Abu's parents. It went on like this. About two years later, Zarina became mother. She gave birth a lovely son. Ishaq's happiness knew no bounds. He gave feasts to relatives and neighbors. Nuts were distributed among the poors. Slowly six months passed.
One day when everyone was sleeping, there was a loud bang.
The bombing was carried out by American and allied forces. Part of the house got broken. A fire broke out. The area where Abu Ishaq's parents, uncle and aunt were sleeping caught fire after the blast.

—".....Father! Mother....!"

Abu Ishaq ran screaming. Zarina also went running behind him. Together, they ceased out the fire. Debris removed, but by then it was too late. Both his father & mother were killed in the attack. Abu's uncle and aunt also perished. Their dead bodies did not get the shroud and burial either. That bodies got burnt in the fire itself.

When Abu and Zarina went out for help, they saw the same   situation was at many places throughout the village. There was fire everywhere. There was chaos. There was a plume of smoke in the sky and a pile of debris on the ground. People were screaming and running towards sometimes here, sometimes there.

Now this happening was started. Sometimes a bomb would fall in that village, sometimes a missile. The people of the village dug a moat in the backyard of their respective houses. Now, whenever the siren of the attack sounded, everyone would hide in it.

Then, the news came that the American and other forces had conquered. The dictator was hanged. A new government was formed. Hoping that everything would be alright. But this did not happen. When the old snake died, a new snake took birth.

The terrorists formed a group IS. They would attack and loot oil wells, banks etc. About ten large oil wells of Iraq and Syria came under their control. Those who bought cheap oil from IS started smuggling it to different countries. Terrorists would take the women hostage, and then get them to the business of prostitution. Gradually, they started attacking different parts of the country and taking them under their control.

One such night, terrorists attacked the village of Abu Ishaq.

Abu and Zarina were sleeping at that time. The child was sleeping too. Abu heard some noise outside. He was surprised. Then, he heard the sound of knocking on the door.

Abu was about to ask whereabouts of the person outside the door, but suddenly Zarina sensed the danger. She stopped him. Then she shouted herself-
—"...who?... who is it?"

A voice came from outside-
—"Open the door, or we'll break it."

Zarina replied-
—"My husband is not at home. I won't open."

Again a voice came from outside -
—"Open, otherwise we'll break."

Zarina whispered and took Abu to the inner room. told-
—"I am feeling threat, take the child and go through the back door."

Abu objected-
—"No, we'll go together. Will live together and die together."

Zarina explained to him-
—"No, we can't run away together, I've heard that terrorists of ISIS kill men and children. We will run separately. I will not be able to run fast with the child. So you take him and run away."

Abu was very worried-
—"But I can't leave you here alone."

By then the sound of breaking the door started coming. thak thak…. The door was old, but of strong wood. So the terrorists were taking time to break it.

Zarina cried again-
—"Do not be mad. Run quickly, when the hazard is over, we will meet again here."

Both exited through the back door, ran off.

The terrorists entered in the house as soon as the door was broken. Not finding anyone in the house, they got furious. After they looted the valuables of the house, they set the whole house on fire.

Many people of the village went to run away to wherever. Many women of the village were taken as hostage. Zarina was one of them. Abu had escaped, but Zarina could not go far. It was a good thing, that she had driven Ishaq away with his son on her oath. What do they do? Who could fight the terrorists? Even after going a long way, Abu could hear gunshots and explosions behind him. Ishaq ran all night with his son. It felt as if death was behind him and if he had stopped, he would have lost. His son would cry on his speedy steps. He would somehow silenced his son, then again started running.

In the morning, Ishaq reached to another city. IS had not reached there yet. He was not getting understand anything. He was gasping badly. He drank water from a nearby tap and washed his hands and face. By then the child started crying. Perhaps, he too was hungry and thirsty. In a panic, Abu could not even take any money.

He knocked at the door of a house in front of him. A voice came from inside-
—"Who is it?"

Abu begged-
—"My baby is very hungry. Will I get some milk? I don't have money."

The owner of the house opened the door murmuring-
—"In the very morning, they come to beg."

But then, the heart of the owner of the house melted at the sight of the child. He called the house maid. To feed the child, Abu got some camel's milk. Abu sat there by the door and started feeding the child.

The owner of the house investigated-
—"whether the child is of theft?"

Ishaq narrated his story with tears.
—"No! Our village was attacked. Some were killed, some were taken as hostage. With great difficulty, I ran for my life."

—"Where is his mother?"

—"I don't know, we ran separately to save our lives. We got separated."
Abu started crying while telling this.

The owner of the house felt pity. On side of his house, a building was being constructed. At the same, Abu got a job as a laborer. He would give the child to the maid of the house, who would look after him. He was very much worried about Zarina. Do not know what the oppressors must have done to her, whether she was alive or dead. But now he did not even have the courage to return back to his village.

There, in the village the young men were collected and taken away in vans. They were later sold as slaves. Children, old people who were not in a condition to do any work, they all made stood in straight line and were shot by the terrorists. The bullet went through the body by body, hit the next second standing in the line, then the third. Bullets were expensive for those terrorists, there was no value for human life.
Such was the state of savagery that they even mutilated the corpses to the fullest, as if practicing butchery. Houses and shops were looted and then set on fire.
Zarina and other women were captured by IS. They were taken to an unknown place. A man was employed

to sort out the women. They were then stripped naked and brought to a market. There were a large number of women on the top of the platform. Their hands were tied. There stood a bald man, with a white beard. He had a whip in his hand. There was wickedness showing from his face.

Standing on a stone, he was making a sound, just as the fruit-vegetable sellers in the market makes-

—"Take beautiful women, tender women of good families. Have a mistress, get married. Make them prostitute, earn money."

There were a lot of buyers gathered there. Who were measuring the parts of women's body with their lustful eyes. Some would even inflict bruise with their hands.

The women were very scared. Those whose face and even hair were earlier covered with hijab and burqa, were now being auctioned without clothes.

Waving his whip in between, the bald man would even whack any of women. When red mark was made on her tender body, he would ask for a higher price by calling her a mild-lady.

Those women were bid by the buyers. Those who were beautiful were bought and put in the business of prostitution. And those who were ordinary in appearance were sold as domestic slaves. The rest were sent to camps to pacify the lust of the terrorist fighters. The women who were found pregnant, were forcibly aborted by the terrorists. Those who had young children, those children were either killed after snatching them from the mothers, or beaten heavily in front of the woman, so that the women were forced to accept slavery.

Since Zarina had also become a mother once, she did not get good money in the auction. But seeing her beauty, she too was taken as a slave in a camp. About 175 to 200 women were brought in the camp. They also belonged to the same community to which Zarina belonged. They were not given anything to eat or drink for the first 2 days. The women had become weak, suffering from hunger and thirst. Then they were raped. Hungry and thirsty women did not have enough power to resist it.

On refusal by a woman, her one year old child was taken away. Then she was given meat and rice, as food on that day. Everyone was surprised because there was only salt being given along with the rice in the camp to inmates. The woman refused to eat without taking her child back. The terrorist told her that if she eats the food, he will bring her child and give it to her.

When the woman ate the food, the terrorist said-
—"We have cooked your one-year-old son, which we took from you, and this is what you have eaten."
The woman roared in anger and sorrow and started crying. Then in the morning it was learned that, out of pain and self-indulgence, she committed suicide.

In the camp, the atrocities on women continued unabated. Sometimes they had to pacify the lusts of many terrorists in one night. There was no question to protest. Terrorists with whips, would peel off their skins immediately. Many a times women fainted after suffering torture.

Some women were trained and sent into cities as suicide bombers. They would be sent to a crowded market, wearing a jacket filled with explosives. A henchman would accompany them. Upon reaching there, the woman would be blown away by pressing a button on the remote by the henchman.

A few days later, the terrorists came to know that Zarina was a nurse. The terrorists first put her to look after care of other women's health. It also included pregnancy screening and abortion of women. Fearing to save her life, Zarina agreed to do the same. Later, some terrorists also started coming to her to get the bandage done. But in spite of all this, her position was never better than any other woman in the camp.

Once the terrorists kidnapped and brought two journalists. Their names were George and Fernandez. The journalist, George, had received a bullet in the leg. He was screaming in pain that-

— "kill me, kill me".

The Masked terrorist ordered to call Zarina. They caught Zarina and brought her. The masked man asked-

—"Can you cure him? He got a gunshot in the leg."

Zarina replied-

—"I have treated the bullet shots in the past, but he looks injured very much. It would be better to take him to the hospital."

The masked man grabbed Zarina's hair. Zarina groaned in pain. The masked man shouted-

—"I didn't ask you for your advice. You will have to treat him, he just shouldn't die."

Zarina started the treatment of that journalist George. She heated the knife and then began to eject the bullet with the help of the same. With no anesthesia available, the journalist kept shouting-

—"Don't you have anesthetics. Ahh! Ahh!"

Zarina told him-

—"No, it's out of stock."

The journalist groaned in pain and asked-

—"by what time, will it come back to stock?"

—"I don't know. You should cooperate me otherwise, if anything happens to you, they will beat me."

Barely, the bullet came out.

The journalist heaved a sigh of relief. Then questioned-
—"Who are you? Are you one of them, or have these people also grabbed you from somewhere?"

Zarina thought for a while and told the journalist about herself-
—"I am the unlucky one…. These people attacked and destroyed my entire village. The young men were collected and carried away in vans. They were later sold as slaves. The rest were lined up and shot dead. Among the women, who were beautiful, they were bought into the sex trade and those who were ordinary in appearance were sold as domestic slaves. The rest were brought to the camps here to pacify the lust of the terrorist fighters."

The treatment lasted for several days. Every day George was brought to her to be bandaged. During the treatment, Zarina told him about herself. She told him about her husband and child. George would go and tell all that to another journalist, Fernandez, who was with him in captivity.
One day, it was afternoon. Hot winds were blowing. The terrorists either had some suspicion, or their demand was not accepted, they decided to kill George. They caught George and took him to a hill. A henchman was holding a video camera in his hand. Video recording was going on. The journalist was dressed in orange clothes. The journalist understood that these people were going to kill him. He fell at their feet and started crying and begging for life.
Zarina was also caught and taken away. She felt that the journalist had informed them about the conversation with Zarina. She started trembling with fear. She fell at the feet of the terrorists and started pleading-

—"Leave me, don't kill me, I beg you for my life."

A terrorist assured her that she would not be killed. There a sword was handed over to Zarina on the hill. The masked man told her-
—"If you want your life to be safe, you will have to kill this journalist."

Zarina got scared. said-
—"….. I… how can I kill him? I haven't killed anyone earlier. I cannot do this."

Putting a gun on Zarina's forehead, the terrorist said-
—"Either you kill him, or I will kill you."

Zarina had never killed anyone before. Her hands started trembling. She closed her eyes. In her mind, her husband and son appeared. To meet them, she had to be alive. She wielded the sword.

But the sword did not hit the journalist's neck with full force. The neck was not separated from the torso, but the wound was still deep, and the journalist, screaming loudly, fell to the ground and started agonizing.
The terrorists showing the agonizing George, made some threats and speeches before the camera. By the end of the video, the journalist died in agony. Later that video was released on the internet, which showed their brutality.
That night, Zarina had gone almost mad. The hand that saved lives in the hospital, had killed a human being. Again and again, the agony of the journalist would come in her mind, and she would start crying. Her whole body starts trembling.
After the video of the gruesome murder of a journalist was circulated, the government swung into action. The second journalist, Fernandez, was released after

considerable bargaining, in exchange for several million dollars and the release of some of the terrorists captured by the allied forces.

Upon the release of the journalist Fernandez, the US military took him into custody and began to inquire about the whereabouts of the terrorists.
A reconnaissance plane was sent to the valley of Mount Caesar on the trails of the journalist. Seeing the reconnaissance aircraft, one of the terrorists guarding there shouted something in secret language, and he alerted everyone. Everyone went and hid in the bunkers.

But after this incident, the atrocities on Zarina started increasing. The terrorists suspected that she had told something to the journalists. They stopped giving her food. The chief terrorist asked her-
—"We suspect that you have told the journalist a lot about this location. It is in your own interest to tell the truth, what have you told him?"

—"But I haven't told him anything."
Zarina replied. Her face had turned pale.

The main terrorist told his comrades-
—"She will not obey like this. We have to treat her."
He gestured by shaking his hand.

A terrorist came forward. He tore off all of Zarina's clothes and stripped her. Then, dragged her away and tied her to a nearby pole. Then two terrorists arrived with leather belts in their hand. They started beating Zarina with their belts by turns. Zarina started screaming in pain.

She exhausted due to pain and got fainted. Thereafter, she was released back into the bunker. But from then, she was subject to constant torture. Many of people would rape her throughout the night, they used to keep beating her. She was asked what she had told to the reporters.

One night a drone passed by, and dropped some bombs. But they fell in the wrong places, due to which there was no significant damage. It seemed that the drone was not aware of the target, and was dropping bombs based on conjecture. There was a rush due to the bombing. The terrorist who was with Zarina at that time quickly put on his clothes, picked up his gun and fled outside. In a flurry, he forgot to tie Zarina. Zarina felt that this was the right time. She put on her clothes and covertly she came out of the bunker, and then she ran aside. There was a canal there. A terrorist saw her. He ran towards her. He shouted-
—"Stop, or else I'll shoot you."

Zarina's life had become worse than death there. Zarina had decided that now she has to get rid of all this, whether she lives alive or not. Her steps did not stop.

She went and jumped into the canal. The canal was deep. But her foot hit a stone in the canal and she screamed. Perhaps, she had broken a bone in her leg. Well, at the same time the terrorist opened fire to her, but it did not hit her. But when the terrorist heard her scream, he thought that Zarina had been shot with the bullet, and he returned away.
On the other hand, through the journalist, the US-Iraqi military had come to know who Zarina's husband was. They, with the help of their spies, traced him. He was arrested and taken to jail. They suspected that he too was involved with the terrorists. They tortured him so that he would reveal the address of his wife, who had killed an international journalist. They asked Abu-

—"Look, Abu, your wife has killed an international journalist. We are looking for her. You tell us where is she?"

Abu replied-
—"I don't know, both of us had escaped after the attack on our village. Then, we got separated. I do not know where she is, in what condition, she is alive or dead, I do not know anything."

An officer said-
—"he won't tell, hang him upside down."

Abu was hanged upside down. Then he was hit hard by them. He kept shouting helplessly-
—"Have mercy on me. Have mercy on me, spare me for God's sake. I don't know anything."

Then Abu was taken down. They tore his clothes, and Abu was made lied on an iron bed naked. Then, electric shocks were given to him. He kept screaming and begging for mercy, soon he fainted thereafter. But he did not know anything, so he could not tell anything. This went on for several days.

Here, while flowing in the drain, Zarina reached a pond. There she cleansed herself. Then, taking the support of a wooden stick, she traveled further. She had to find her husband and child. But first, she had to get her broken leg treated. Somehow, while walking, she reached a village. She begged and ate something there. Then she went to the primary health center of that village. There was a nurse sitting at the reception. She was working on some papers with her face down. Zarina told the nurse-
—"listen."

The nurse looked up at her face. Zarina was standing with the help of wood. Her face had turned black. The old clothes were dirty and torn all over the place.
Zarina told her-
—"I have broken a bone in my leg, I have to get treatment."

 The nurse started making the slip-
—"Name?"

—" Zarina, Zarina Abu Ishaq."

—"Age?"

—"Twenty five years."

—" How did your leg get broken?"

—"I had fallen in the drain."

But seeing her condition, the nurse was thinking something else. The nurse questioned her a lot. Zarina thought for a while and told the nurse her story. In no time, the doctor came. He put Zarina's bone in place and applied plaster on her leg. Then he went back to the other room to see the patients.
Then, the nurse started preparing an injection. Since Zarina was herself a nurse, she read the name of the medicine written on the vial. It was an anesthetic. She asked-
—"What medicine is this?"

The nurse told-
—"It is Pain killer. You will get rest."

Zarina said-
—"You're lying, it's anesthetic."

Nurse said-
—"Oh no...You're getting it wrong."

When Zarina protested, the nurse tried to inject her forcefully. Zarina twisted the hand of the nurse and gave the injection to the nurse by own hands of the nurse. Zarina was lucky that there was no one else in the room at that time.

By the time, Zarina recalled that the terrorists were making videos when she killed the journalist. Maybe that video, they would have put it on the internet. That's why the nurse might be trying to make her unconscious. Probably, she would made her unconscious and hand her over to the police.
Zarina ran away from there. She pleaded at a local Motel. The owner of the Motel was a kind person. He gave Zarina the work of washing the dishes there. She started getting food and some money there.
Here, when the soldiers were convinced that Abu Ishaq did not know anything about his wife, they got his beseeching message broadcasted on behalf of Abu in newspapers, on TV and in other media-
—"...Zarina, I am Abu Ishaq speaking. I am alive and our son is also well. Wherever you are, surrender to the police. These people will make you meet to me."

Zarina was washing dishes that day. She heard Abu Ishaq's message on the radio. When Zarina came to know that her husband was alive and her son was also alive, she surrendered herself to the police.
Since Zarina herself had fled from the terrorist camp, she told the army about the exact details of the terrorists, routes, numbers, and bunkers. On her trails, the army raided Mount Caesar and freed around 170 women.

Her village was still occupied by ISIS. Army attacked also there and drove the terrorists away.
But the village was completely destroyed. All the men were either killed or sold. A lot of Women were also sold. All the houses were destroyed by bombs and fire.

Zarina was accused for the murder of the journalist, but in circumstances in which she was compelled to commit the murder, she was sentenced for a term of only one year jail. Later, seeing her good behavior in prison, she was pardoned after only six months.
Grieving Zarina and Ishaq decided to move to another city in Iraq. There they took a house on rent and started living as a laborer. Even today, Zarina get shudder by Recalling the atrocities of the IS camp. She doesn't know how she endured all this. Perhaps it was the hope of meeting to her husband and child that kept her alive.
Zarina and Ishaq still hope that their villagers will return one day and once again, their village will be populated and then they will return to their village.

CHAPTER 2
IN THE CLUTCHES OF THE DRAGON

His name was Hing Ching and he was a scientist by profession. He was working in a world-class lab in Wuhan, China.

This lab was created to conduct scientific tests on various bacteria, viruses and diseases caused by them. The lab was very modern. Quite big and beautifully made. Modern machines and tools were there. The people working there used to get well paid.

When Hing Ching started his job, he was told that this lab tested drugs and bacterial viral diseases. Gradually, he became a part of that lab. Hing Ching was very intelligent. Everyone in the lab was extremely happy with his work.

One day, he was called over the intercom by his team supervisor Chao Jedang. He asked-
—"Hello, Hing, how are you?"

Hing Ching replied-
—"Fine sir."

Chao Jedang told him-
—"Well, there is good news for you, that you have been selected for the virus testing team."

Hearing this, Hing Ching's eyes shined up. This was a promotion for Hing Ching. An important opportunity to learn with a increase in salary. He thanked his supervisor very happily.

He hung up the phone. His heart was throbbing with joy. He informed his section colleagues-
—"Listen, there is good news and a bad one, which one will you listen first?"

A colleague said-

—"the good one."

Hing Ching said with joy,
—"The good news is that I have been promoted. The bad news is that I have to leave this section and go to the virus testing team."

Colleagues congratulated him-
—"Wow, Hing Ching, many many congratulations, now tell me, when are you giving the treat to us?"

Hing Ching said-
—"today itself."

Hing Ching voiced Mr. George. Mr. George was the canteen owner there, who provided food, snacks and drinks for everyone.
—"Mr. George, Mr. George, bring us refreshments for everyone. Classy soup, meat balls and chicken noodles please. And of course, beer to drink along."

Mr. George laughed and said-
—"I will bring it in no time."

In about half an hour, all the food and drink items arrived. Everyone enjoyed a lot and praised the food.

After this, Hing Ching called over phone his wife Ming Ching and told-
—"Ming, listen, don't cook supper tonight. We're going out to eat."

Ming Ching asked-
—"Why, is there anything special?"

Hing Ching told her-
—"Yes, there is a good news, I have been promoted."

—"Wow, when did this happen?"
Ming was overjoyed to hear that.

Hing Ching said-
—"Just got the information a while back. You be ready in the evening."

—"Okay."

When he got home, he stopped the car. His Wife Ming Ching and his three-year-old daughter Miao Ching, both sat ready. Hing Ching made them sit in the car and took them out for dinner.
It was an expensive hotel in China. Hing Ching was wearing his favorite suit that day. Ming Ching was wearing a top and skirt. Miao was wearing a frock and was looking lovely.
All three sat in the cabin inside the restaurant. It was solitude there. The waiter brought the water and the menu card. Hing ching and his wife ordered food of their choice.
Miao ordered the pudding, which she liked the most. Ming moved the pudding to Miao-
—"Take daughter, pudding for you."

Miao urged-
—"I will eat with hands of dad."

Hing Ching made her sit on his lap, and started feeding her the pudding.

Hing told Ming-
—"Now we will get our flat from the government, and we will get rid of the landlord's squabble."

Ming said happily-

—"Oh wow! our own flat?"

—"Yes, because bacteriological testing is very top secret job, the government keeps the scientists separate from the common people. So that no information could be leaked."

—"Well, what about salary, will that increase too?"

—"Yes."

—"How much?"

Hing Ching guessed and said-
—"Almost twice."

—"Wow! I have to buy jewelery and new clothes too."
Ming Ching began to calculate in her mind, what she would buy from the first salary.

—"Everything will be bought, let the salary come first."

Then Ming Ching joked.
—"But don't make yourself sick with bacteria and viruses. Ha ha ha ha."

—"Hey…ha…ha, oh no, a lot of protection are given to the scientists working there."

After the meal, they started going back. Hing tipped the waiter. He was very happy that day.

On the second day, Hing was made to join his new department. This lab used to process bacteria and viruses. Then they test them on humans. After infecting them, they treat them with medicines.

For Hing Ching, it was a humanitarian act. Study of diseases and discovery of drugs to control diseases. Hing Ching had found a luxurious cabin there. Beautiful blue walls, beautiful glass table. He started working there diligently.

For the experiments, they used to get volunteers, who were often poor men, who came under the greed of money. Or the criminals serving a prison sentence, which would have been provided by the government.

Then gradually, a whole colony of those volunteers was established there. Among them were children, women, men, old people. They were provided accommodation with a tin shed houses. Who were they, why they were brought there? Those unlucky volunteers were not aware at all.

Hing Ching's team was told that in order to keep the experiments a secret, it should not be discussed the volunteers at all that tests are going on them.

Well, Hing Ching had nothing to do with it. He only wanted to perform his duty.

The story of criminals settled there by the government, or rather say that the government considered them to be criminals, begins about two years ago.

########

Location - One of the camps built to keep the Uyghur Muslims imprisoned, Xinjiang province....

This camp was not just a camp. It was a very large, three-storied paved, cluster of two buildings, with lawn kitchens, classrooms and a number of cells for keeping prisoners. There were two separate buildings for men and women. There was tight security throughout the building, CCTV cameras were installed, even in the inmates' bathrooms.

There, the guards were always wearing masks. They were seen wearing a special red and yellow suit. They were not in police uniform.

At any time after midnight, they would enter the cell and pick up any of women. These people dragged them through the corridor and took them to the 'dark room'. In the 'Dark Room' those women would be subjected to horrific atrocities.

China said that these camps were set up to "re-educate" the Uyghur people and people of other minority communities.

While it was human rights organizations' saying that, the Chinese government has gradually taken away religious and other freedoms of the Uyghur people. Now, they were collectively monitored. Now and then, they were taken into custody without any notice. The religious leaders of the Uyghur people were forcibly made to dance on erotic songs. The women there, who previously wore traditionally long and covered dresses, their clothes would be cut short in public now. They are not allowed to wear naqab(mask) and hijab(scarf). Their religious freedom was banned. And the food items which were forbidden in their religion, they were forced to eat them. Attempts were made to change their mind and even forced sterilization was done to stop their population growth.

This campaign was started by the President of China against the Uyghur people. In year 2014, there were extremist attacks by Uyghur separatists in Xinjiang. Leaked documents reveal that since then, China had instructed its officials to 'show no mercy' at all to Uyghurs and teach them a lesson.

'Khalida Un Chan' lived with her husband 'Ibrahim Un Chan' in a village at Xinjiang province. Ibrahim Un Chan had a meat shop there. His family in Xinjiang came from the Uyghurs Muslim community. He used to have a happy family there. Their house was small but well built. His shop was also in the fore part of the house.

Ibrahim had small eyes and a flat nose, as typical of Chinese people, but was distinguished by a distinctively traditional beard. He also used to wear the traditional cap for his prayers. Khalida also used to wear gowns etc. like other Chinese women. But she used to wear a scarf, as she was taught at her home.

Their village was dominated by Uyghur community. Everyone would go to the mosque together, for offering Prayers.

Ibrahim would sell meat to fulfill needs of the village. He used to do his work with utmost sincerity. Perfect weight, right price and fresh stuff. Everyone respected him. There was no wealth in the house, but there was enough money and satisfaction to live life well.

Everyone was passing own life happily in the village. There, some would do farming, some minor employment or work in the factory.

In year 2014, there were extremist attacks by Uyghur separatists in Xinjiang. Since then, bad days have come for the residents of Xinjiang province.

The Chinese government did the research. According to that research, the Uyghur community was religiously quite different from the Chinese people, and they might, perhaps, demand a separate country in the name of religion.

It was decided that the Uyghur community should be religiously degraded so that they find their thinking and traditions rubbish. For this special training camps were recommended. It was decided that they should be made loyal to the Chinese Empire.

Their population should be controlled and reduced gradually. For this, sterilization campaigns were started.

They were removed from Xinjiang and displaced in many other parts of the country so that they could not unite. Media and tele-communication were banned.

Gradually, the religious and other freedoms of the Uyghur people were taken away. They could no longer offer prayers in the open. Forcibly, their religious leaders were arrested and forced to dance and sing, which was against their traditional beliefs.

Women were forced to wear short clothes. The policemen would stand in the market, the woman whose skirt seemed long to them, they would cut their clothes publicly on the spot with scissors. Hijab, religious cap and masks were banned. Now, they were being monitored collectively. Now and then, they were taken into custody and sent to training camps. Attempts were made to change their mind and even they were sterilized forcefully.

The villagers were upset and scared. Those who protested were either imprisoned or they disappeared mysteriously.

One day a team of Chinese police raided the village of Khalida and Ibrahim. Ibrahim was sipping tea sitting at home that time. He heard some noise outside. He was surprised. Then, sound of knocking came at the door of Ibrahim's house.

Ibrahim asked-

—".....who... who is it?"

A voice came from outside-

—"Police! Open the door, or we'll break it."

Ibrahim said in a nervous tone-

—"No wait, I'm opening."

As soon as the door was opened, the police came in hurriedly. They grabbed Khalida and Ibrahim by the neck and pushed them out.

Ibrahim started pleading-
—"Tell me so, what is our fault, where are you taking us?"

The policemen didn't bother to answer anything.

Ibrahim was surprised to see the scene outside. Many vans were parked outside. Perhaps, they had arrested the whole village.

They put the men in separate vans and the women in separate vans. Everyone was blindfolded so that they could not know where they were being taken. They were taken in the van to a camp. There were two buildings. Men were taken to the building meant for men while women were taken to the second building. There were many soldiers in the camp. They searched everyone.

In the camp, all the women had to take off their jewellery. Khalida's earrings were pulled out. Blood started pouring out of her ears.

Khalida started crying in pain-
—"If you had to take earrings, you would have said, I would have given them. Why is it drawn like this? There's so much bleeding."

The guard growled-
—"It's rule, no jewelry, no mask."

They were taken from there and put in a room where some women were already imprisoned.

The security guards at the camp pulled off a cloth tied on a woman's head. The woman who was wearing a long dress, her dress was torn in half on the spot. Hairs of women were forcibly cut and shortened.

Later, the women were asked to hand over their shoes and all clothing fitted with buttons and elastic to the soldiers. They were given a separate dress to wear there. After this, they were taken to the cells made in different blocks.
Nothing happened for the first couple of months. Simply, they were forced to watch China's propaganda program in the cell. But later the atrocities escalated.
There were ten women in Khalida's cell. They were given a thin mattress and blanket to sleep on the ground.
One night Khalida and the women of her cell were preparing to sleep. A woman who slept next to her in the cell told her that she had been brought there for having much children. Khalida asked curiously-
—"what is your name?"

—"Saba."

—"How many children do you have?"

—"two."

—"Two is not much."

—"These people told that according to the law, there can be only one child."

—"Where is your husband?"

She smiled-

—"When they all raided at our house, I made my husband run away with the kids."
She didn't have tension that she was in captivity or that bad things were going to happen to her, she was only satisfied that her husband and children would be safe.
Then, one day at twelve o'clock in the night, some guards came, they grabbed Saba's arm and said-
—"Come on, it's your turn today!

Saba was terribly nervous. She started crying-
—"Leave me, where are you taking me, what will you do with me?"

But they forcefully took her away. She remained missing for three days. Three days later, when she returned, scars were all over her body. She was in a deranged condition. she was not able say anything. Everyone was shocked seeing her condition.

Khalida asked-
—"What happened? How did that marks happen to you?"

In response, Saba's voice was not coming out of her mouth, she was sobbing incessantly by putting her arm around Khalida's neck. She was unable to speak anything.

Khalida made her drink water. Then Saba, told her in sobbing and crying.
They asked her about the address of her husband. She was beaten a lot for not telling. Then, they raped her. But where was her husband, in what condition was he, she herself did not have the news, so how would the poor woman tell.

Khalida consoled her. Then, both of them hugged together and started crying. Khalida looked up at the sky and prayed. She started worrying about her husband.

After that, the game of those guards started. One or the other woman was picked up from the cell every night. She was taken to the dark room. There a woman, named Suyang was deployed. She used to sit at the reception. Suyang's job was to take off the women's clothes and handcuff them so that they could not move. Thereafter, she would leave them in the room and leave. After this, those women were raped by a man wearing a mask. Sometimes, women were also gang raped. If a woman opposed it, she would be beaten up or she would be given shock with the electric shock rod.
Then, when the men inside the room left, Suyang would take the woman to bathe.
Chinese men who came there, paid Suyang money to present the youngest and most beautiful of those female prisoners.

Some of the women were taken from the cell to somewhere else at night. Only a few of them returned. The rest did not come back. No one knew where they went. The women who had returned to the cell, were told not to tell anyone what happened to them.
No one was allowed to tell what happened to them. One could just lie there silently. All this was being done to crush the soul of every prisoner there. Their faith, self-respect, self-confidence were all being eroded.

One day, Khalida and a 20-25 year old woman living in her cell were also taken out. They were first presented in front of a Chinese male wearing a mask. On his orders, the woman who was with her, was taken to another room.

The Chinese man wearing a mask asked Khalida to be taken to the dark room.
Suyang took Khalida to the next room. Some soldiers were also inside. Seeing them, Khalida got horrified. spoke-
—"Why have you brought me here? What do you want to do with me? Let me go."

A soldier scolded her, said-
—"Stand quietly."

Suyang took off all of Khalida's clothes and began to handcuff her.
Those soldiers had an Electrified rod in their hands. Khalida tried to sit on the ground in resistance and self-defense, but the man threw an electric current at her by touching her back with electrified rod. She had to stand up due to shock and pain.
Khalida was also subjected to what happened with other women there. All that happened with Khalida too. She was tortured. She was gang raped several times. Each time, two or three men raped her.
One day her condition got very bad and she started bleeding profusely. She started screaming in intense pain. Then she fainted.
Khalida's torture in the dark room ended that night when Suyang, who had brought her there, told the mask man that Khalida's condition was getting worse and that, Khalida needed medical help.
They took Khalida to the doctor at the camp. Khalida was moaning in pain and she could not even stand.
A doctor at the camp said that Khalida may have got an internal wound due to rape, which was causing internal bleeding. When the woman living with Khalida in her cell, told the doctor that Khalida was bleeding profusely, The doctor replied that it was normal. Women have bleeding, sometimes it becomes more. However,

Khalida was given a pain killer medicine. After that she was sent back to her cell.

Apart from the cells and dark rooms built in these camps, one more thing was significant. And those were the classrooms built there. Yellow and red walls, iron benches. There, teachers were appointed to 're-educate' these prisoners. There was a daily ongoing lectures there. The traditional customs and religious practices of the Uyghur people were described as orthodox. Those teachers criticized Uyghur's traditions severally. It was a process of snatching away the culture, language and religion of the Uyghur and other minorities, and infusing them into mainstream Chinese culture.

Khalida spent the weeks, then months, living in the camp. The hair of the prisoners living there were cut short. They had to attend the lectures every day.
Apart from this, every woman had to undergo a medical test every week. Nothing was told about why these tests were being conducted. Perhaps to make sure that the woman did not become pregnant due to rape, or some scientific test was being done on them. At a interval of every 15 days, Medicines were forcefully given to them. No one knew what these medicines were for. Sometimes, injections also had to be given.
Women were forced to have installed IUDs (contraceptive devices) or were sterilized so that they could not beget children any more.
Don't know whether they brainwashed those prisoner, or whether it was the effect of injections and medicines, that their mind started going numb. Those prisoners now felt that, to get rid of all this, they would have to sacrifice their religion and culture.
Khalida and other villagers were released in December 2018, not to their home, but in an unknown village. They were left with the people they were with, spoce, children

all. Khalida could not understand this change in the government's policy. However, life got back on track. All the people of the village were settled there.

They were provided with tin shed houses in that unknown village. Khalida and her husband, once again, started their life and business. Entire settlements, shops etc. were resettled. But they were not provided with mobile or telephone facility. They were banned from going out of that village. Even in TV, only government news channels used to come.
Those Villagers had no idea that this village had been built for scientific testing and, like rats and frogs in the labs, they were all about to be subjected to brutal experiments.

######

On the other hand, Hing Ching and his team started research on how the bacteria spread. Especially when, this biological attack is from an enemy country. A large bomb filled with bacteria was dropped on Khalida and Ibrahim's village as an experiment.
But they were disappointed because during the explosion, all the bacteria were killed by the heat of the bomb.
The villagers heard the sound of an explosion that day. People panicked and came out of the houses. A bomb had exploded at an empty field, causing no damage there.

Hing Ching's team was quite disappointed. A scientist from the team said-
—"Regret it, the heat of the bomb destroyed them all."

Another scientist said-

—"We were wrong. How bacteria could survive in the heat of the bomb?"

Hing Ching said-
—"There is a lot of heat in a bomb blast. They could not bear the heat and died."

Then, a member of Hing Ching's team brainstormed. And they mixed the bacteria with the sand. Once again, the bomb was filled with bacteria and dropped on Khalida and Ibrahim's Village as an experiment. This time the experiment was successful. Ultimately, up to fifty percent of the bacteria were able to survive.
This time the disease was spread in the village. Immediately a team of doctors came, and treated everyone and brought them in health. But an old man who had heart disease earlier, was killed. Everyone in Hing Ching's team congratulated each other on the success.

A problem with this research was that, although the bacteria were contagious, they were treatable with normal antibiotics. Also, there was a risk associated with spreading the bacteria with the help of bomb that affected countries may quickly detect it.
Then this research was stopped deeming as unnecessary.
Now their focus was on viruses. Research on this was started afresh.
Viruses are characterized by the fact that they are unicellular microscopic organisms that can reproduce themselves only in a living cell. They are made up of nucleic acids and proteins. They are dead-like outside the body, but they become alive as soon as they enter the body of a living person. The virus can remain dormant for hundreds of years, without any food or water. And whenever the virus comes in contact with a

living person, it penetrates and covers the cell of that person and the person becomes ill.

For this research, a lot of money started coming from the government and volunteers were also provided for research.

Hing Ching sometimes felt that someone may misuse this research. But there was tight security in the lab and everyone had full faith in the government.

But gradually the intention of the Chinese government started changing. They had a high level secret official meeting.

In those days, China was trying to increase its supremacy by threatening the small countries of the South China Sea. Apart from this, it had illegally occupied Tibet, a country as well. Other countries including America, Britain, and Europe were opposing it. Even the International Court of Justice has ruled against China on the issue of the South China Sea.

This enraged China. To teach a lesson to various countries including America, those countries were targeted to commit horrific genocide through the pandemic. By sabotaging the economies of all developed countries, China's economy was targeted for a boost.

It was also expected that after the spread of the disease, other countries would buy medical equipments, kits, vaccines, etc. from China to protect people of those countries, and China's economy would become to number one.

But there was a danger that some country might attack China, accusing it for spreading the disease deliberately. To deal with this, in the meeting of the top officials, it was decided that first a complete team of 1500-2000 people should be prepared. They should be infected by the disease and sent to different countries. All those people will come back to China, after roaming around and spreading the disease in different countries. And then they will be made disease free by administrating vaccine, so that the doubt remains that from where the disease spread?

This time they had to find a disease that would make a man terribly ill and kill him, while also being highly contagious and spreading.

Research was done on the virus of SARS and bats but without success. Then a virus was obtained through reverse genetic engineering.

It was found successful in the initial test. Then its vaccine was also made. Thereafter, it was decided to conduct a detailed test of it.

One day some people came to Khalida's Village, and knocked on the door of Khalida's house. As soon as the door opened, they and the Chinese policemen entered in the house. They took Khalida's husband away. Khalida wondered, were they going to keep him in captivity again? Was he going to be tortured again?

Ibrahim was blindfolded. He was taken to an unknown place. On reaching inside the building, his blindfold was opened. It appeared to be a hospital, or perhaps a laboratory. There was also a morgue. Then, he was taken to a room, where a patient was already lying on the bed. Ibrahim was made to sit beside him. In the meantime, the patient coughed and sneezed two or four times. After about an hour some soldiers came. Ibrahim noticed that now, than before, they covered themselves from top to bottom in special plastic robes and wore face masks. Ibrahim's eye was again blindfolded. He was taken back and released back to his village.

Here, Khalida was sitting at the door worried, when a van stopped before house, they dropped Ibrahim at his house and left from there.

Khalida and Ibrahim were surprised. Why was Ibrahim taken away? Why, then, was brought back safely and left? Why did all the guards and the driver of the van cover themselves with plastic wraps while returning?

In fact, the patient near whom Ibrahim was seated was infected with corona. While Ibrahim was sitting next to him, the patient coughed or sneezed two or three times. Due to this Ibrahim became infected with the virus. Then, soldiers wearing PPE kits went to drop Ibrahim to his village. This was actually done so that the soldiers would not get sick themselves.

But a few days after this incident, Ibrahim himself became ill. And at the same time many people in his village also became ill. Initially they had a cough, cold, and fever. But soon, all of them started having trouble in breathing. This infection was spread only through Ibrahim. The medical team came and all the patients were made admitted to the hospital.

This test was very successful. Despite serious and all possible treatment, all those infected people died. Among them, one was the unfortunate Ibrahim. But Khalida survived by chance. Do not know how? Corpses were piled up. The relatives of the patient were in a bad condition by crying. Someone's mother or father was dead, someone's husband, someone's son or daughter. Somewhere, the whole family was wiped out.

Now was the time to implement the second phase of the plan. A complete team of 1500-2000 people was created. Their members were sent to different countries after being infected by the disease. All of them roamed around different places of different countries of the world and then came back. Then, all of them were made cured out of the disease.

Gradually the whole world came under the grip of the disease. People started dying fast. Some people from China also got infected with the disease, but due to medicines and vaccines within their reach, very few people died in China.

When different countries did not think of any solution, they imposed a lockdown on their own.

Meanwhile, China started selling PPE kits, masks, medicines etc. The world economy came to a standstill, but the Chinese economy shone.

Hing Ching was having breakfast in the morning. Ming Ching had prepared his favorite omelet and apple juice, along with butter toast.

TV was on. News was going on.

"China's economy has registered a growth of 58.3% compared to last year. This is the biggest jump in China's gross domestic product (GDP) since 1992.

However, the figures released on Friday did not meet to the expectations, which according to economists of Chinese government, should have increased by 59%."

Then, international news started coming in. Death figures.....

Crying people.... Burning pyres, burial of dead.

Seeing all this, Hing Ching felt dizzy.

That day, he was not feeling well in the office. He tried to talk to his senior officers in this matter, but they advised him to keep quiet, calling it a state matter. When he became a scientist, he thought that he would make great inventions which would benefit humanity. But he had created the virus of a disease, which was going to eat humanity. In the evening he left for his house by car. He was immersed in thought. He started thinking to himself-

—"Oh, what have I done…."

Hing Ching was feeling regretful for his actions. Due to his, many people died in the world. At night he started having scary dreams. While sleeping at night, he would suddenly wake up screaming. Every now and then, he went to the bathroom and would start washing his hands. He felt that his hands are stained with blood.

Seeing him upset, Ming became worried, asked-
—"You look so upset, what's the matter?"

Hing looked at her and hung his face. What would he tell her?
Ming further asked-
—"And why do you keep washing your hands all the time?"

Looking at his hands, Hing Ching said-
—"Look Ming, what the stains are on these hands, it does not leave."

Ming while holding his hand said-
—"Hing, show me."

Ming took the Hing's hands in her hands and looked upside and back of them. There was no stain. Ming said-
—"There is nothing."

—"Why not, look at these, these stains, these are blood stains."

Ming was horrified. She shouted-
—"Hing, Hing, have you gone mad? Come to your senses."

Hing was crying badly.

One night, Hing was sleeping. In the dream he felt that his daughter Miao was calling him-
—"Dad, papa, take me in your arms!"

Hing spread his arms to take her in his lap. Suddenly, a huge and scary dragon came throwing fire from its mouth and ate his baby girl.

He broke his sleep in panic. He was sweating, and was gasping profusely. A jug of water and a glass was lying on his side table. With trembling hands, he grabbed the jug and drank all the water of the jug in one breath.
He looked at Miao. She was sleeping. He took her in his lap and then on his shoulder. But what's this! Miao had a high fever.

Leigh Sung was a pediatrician. He was among best friends of Hing Ching. Hing Ching's baby girl, Miao Ching, had become seriously ill. He took her to Leigh Sung. Hing Ching told Leigh Sung about Miao's fever-
—"Leigh Sung, please see, Miao suddenly got a high fever."

Leigh Sung took out the stethoscope and said-
—"Don't worry, I see."

Leigh Sung conducted a health check-up on Miao. Then various types of pathological tests were conducted. Then, Leigh Sung said-
—"Friend, I have to say with regret that Miao is suffering with Corona."

Hing Ching was assured. He took Miao Chung to the medical team of his laboratory. Treatment was started but it was too late, the infection had spread throughout lungs of Miao. Miao was put on a ventilator. Till five days, Miao was on a ventilator. On the sixth day, Hing Ching was informed that Miao had died. The body was burnt by the medical team itself.

Hing Ching went to Leigh Sung crying. Spoke-
—"......This is the all result of my own sins, Leigh,..... Leigh... I took the life of my child with my own hands."

Leigh Sung made him drink water. He thought Hing Ching was grumbling due to the shock of the child's death, but it was not so. After some relaxing, Hing Ching told the whole story to his friend.
Leigh Sung was stunned on hearing this. Spoke-
—"What are you saying this? How did you do that? So many people are dying all over the world, do you know?"

Leigh Sung, pulling his hair, said-
—"Kill me, give me poison. I am a sinner, an enemy of humanity. I don't deserve to be alive."

At first, hate for Hing Ching arose in the heart of Leigh Sung. But soon, he felt pity on seeing him repenting. Then, they both made some decision.
Both of them wrote an article on Corona's disease, and put it on social media under a Pseudo name. In this article, there were details of the disease virus from its genetic to its creation in the laboratory. A Commotion was started all over the world, as soon as this article went viral. Various countries started accusing China for spreading disease and preparing bio-weapons. There was pressure on China that its laboratory in Wuhan should be investigated by an international agency. China refused to get conducted the investigation, calling it a false case.
But in the meantime, somehow, the government came to know that the article was written by Hing Ching. And the soldiers started searching for Hing Ching. They arrested him and took him to an unknown place. He was made to sit on a chair, his hands and feet were tied. A masked man told him-
— "Hing Ching, you were our favorite scientist, who successfully carried out our plan, but now you have become a threat to us. You tried to leak information. Now you must die."

Then, Hing Ching was given an injection of the virus made by him. He left abandoned there without any medical care. Soon he died. But luckily, they could not know about Leigh Sung. Leigh Sung left the country on time and took refuge in Western countries.

In the meantime, Khalida got the opportunity and she also went to the western country via Kazakhstan.

Leigh Sung opened the secret of Wuhan in the media while Khalida described the oppression going in Xinjiang camps along with bio-trials happened to Uyghurs. Both of them completely busted in the media. But they could not bring any evidence with them, so China denied the allegations.

Gradually the situation improved and different countries developed vaccines for the disease, adopting different methods of treatment. And China's plan to earn billions by selling the vaccine was got stuck.

CHAPTER 3
AN ENTANGLED MURDER CASE

There was a church on the outskirts of the city. Along with the church, there was a cemetery and school, as is usually the case in every church. The church also had its own charitable hospital, which provided health care to the poor people at a low rate. There were three hostels, one for the priests and nuns, the other for the school children. The third hostel was the guest house, which was meant for visitors. There was a lawn all around the hostel in which various florae of flowers were planted. There was a well, which still contained water, but was no longer in use. Each hostel was surrounded by high boundary walls with thorns. There were also security guards at each gate.

The church was full of sisters, nuns and priests. Out of which Sister Mento was working in the hospital there. She lived in hostel for priests and nuns.

One morning, Sister Mento was reported missing. When the sweeper went to her room to sweep, Sister Mento was not there. She was also absent in the daily prayer meetings in the church. The head priest was worried. He called his guard. The guard came, saluted. Then said-
—"Yes sir."

There was concern in the voice of the pastor-
—".....Guard....Guard, where is Sister Mento? She is very punctual, always used to come to the prayer meeting on time. Look, she may not be sick?"

The guard replied-
—"I'll go and see right now, Father."

The guard went to find her, but could not find Sister Mento in her room at the hostel. Not in the garden and also nor in the lawn. The guard asked the guard posted in the hostel there-
—"Hey brother, has sister Mento gone anywhere?"

Nidhi Gupta

The guard posted in the hostel said-
—"No, I didn't see her going out today. She must be in her room."

—"That's the problem, she is not in the room and the door is also open."

The guard posted in the hostel asked-
 —"Did you see her in the kitchen?"
The guard went to the kitchen on the ground floor of the building. Sister Mento may have gone to the kitchen to drink water at night or early in the morning. The refrigerator door in the kitchen was left open, a bottle of water was fell on the floor and one of the Sister Mento's shoe was lying on the ground near the fridge.
The guard went back and informed the pastor-
—"….Father……Father, Sister Mento is nowhere. There is no traces of her whereabouts. She is not in her room, not even in the garden and……and……"
The guard was gasping heavily.

—"And what guard?"
The head priest, startled, asked the guard.

—"I went to the kitchen. The refrigerator door in the kitchen was open, a water bottle had fallen on the floor and one of the Sister Mento's shoe was on the ground near the fridge."

—"Oh my god!"
A line of worry fell on the head of the head priest.

The head priest got apprehensive on hearing all this..
On the orders of the head priest, Sister Mento's disappearance was reported to the police.

The police team arrived by noon. its in-charge was ASI Indrajit. Along with him, there was a sleuth dog. ASI Indrajit called the guard. Asked him-
—"Guard, what happened? Tell me in detail."

The guard told-
—"Sister Mento was nowhere to be seen. Today, she did not even come to the morning prayer meeting. At the behest of Father, I went to find her. First, I went to her room. Then looked at the garden and lawn. She was not there. Then I went to the kitchen. There in the kitchen, the door of the refrigerator was open, a bottle of water had fallen on the floor and near the fridge, one of the Sister Mento's shoe was on the ground."

ASI Indrajit said in a prescriptive tone-
—"Show me the kitchen."

The police went to the kitchen. The dog was released after made him sniff the foot of shoe. The dog barked and immediately ran towards the garden. And went to the well in the garden and stopped. There another pair of shoes was found in the bushes.
Indrajit looked into the well. On peek, Sister Mento's corpse was floating in the water. The body was pulled out from the well with the help of guards and constables. Paperwork of the dead body was done. After this the body was sent for the postmortem.

Interrogation took place side by side. Indrajit called the guard posted in the hostel and asked-
—"Whether you were on duty last night?"

He bowed his head and replied-
—"Yes sir."
—"Did you hear any scream or sound in the night?"

—"No sir."

—"Who was in the hostel last night?"

—"Sister Mento, Father Victor, Father Williams and Sister Emilia. The rest of the priests and nuns had shifted to the new hostel building."

—"New building?"

—"Yes, this building is old. A new building has been built on that side for nuns and priests. These four were not able to shift as of now, as there was furniture work left in their rooms."

—"Has anyone else come besides them?"

—"No, no. Last night only maid who prepares food for the dinner, had come. She left after cooking and feeding everyone."

—"And what about in the morning?"

—"Breakfast and lunch are done in the church itself."

Indrajit checked the register of visitors, but there was no record of any other person coming. The boundary wall was also very high, it was covered with barbed wire. It was almost impossible to get over it.

The post-mortem report arrived the next day. The corpse had two small wounds on her head, which did not lead to death. These injuries were not fatal. Apart from this, there were rubbing marks on the right shoulder and hip, which were probably due to the body being dragged to the well. There was no sign of sexual assault. In the postmortem report, despite all the above mentioned injuries, the cause of death was given as drowning in water.

This was followed by a long series of protracted inquiries and investigations by the police.

Sister Mento has no enmity with anyone. She was a calm-tempered, self-assured woman.

Perhaps due to some reason, she had committed suicide by jumping into the well. In depression, she must have left the fridge door open, and one of her shoes.

Thereafter the death was ruled as suicide and the file was closed.

Various questions were arising in everyone's mind. Nobody could digest the idea of suicide. A person, who jumps into a well to commit suicide, does not leave one of her shoes anywhere else. Also, two small wounds on the head of the dead body recorded in the post-mortem report, how did they form? Apart from this, there were rubbing marks on the right shoulder and hip, which were made by dragging the corpse to the well.

Local nurses and a group of citizens took out a candle procession in the city. The slogan of "Give justice to Sister Mento" reverberated in the city. There was a lot of discussion in the media about the Sister Mento murder case.

The police was later accused of destroying important evidence as to the cause of death. The process of their investigation was long, complicated and unsatisfactory. There was a mismatch of facts in their report at many places. They were accused of corruption, working under pressure. As a result, the case was handed over to the CBI.

One day ASI Inderjit and his senior officer Hemant Pant were sitting together in their office. Hemant Pant was very worried. He told-

—"Sister Mento's case is getting very complicated. I don't know what to do."

Indrajit advised-
—"I say sir, that once again, the investigation will have to be started afresh. Instead of committing suicide, this case has to be looked at with the angle of murder."

It was afternoon. It was time for lunch, but both did not get up. Then the phone rang. The constable's call came on the intercom-
—"Some Mr. Laxmikant wanted to meet you."

—"Send him in. And yes, send three cups of tea too."

Laxmikant was in-charge of CBI. Laxmikant came in. Introduced himself by shaking hands with Hemant Pant-
"I am called Laxmikant. I am in charge of CBI. You must have come to know that the case has been handed over to us."

Hemant gestured him to sit on the chair. Laxmikant sat down. Then said-
—"I have come to investigate the Sister Mento murder case. Please show me the file."

Hemant Pant called for the file. Meanwhile, the canteen man left with three cups of tea. Laxmikant started reading the file seriously. Then started asking-
—"What do you feel? Is it murder or suicide?"

Hemant replied-
—"Prima facie, it is suicide."
Hemant was still adamant on his point. Indrajit stared at Hemant.

Laxmikant raised his eyes-
—"The reason?"

—"Because, there was no reason for the murder. The deceased was a nun. She was also looking after the job of a nurse. Who will be her enemy? But now, we are looking at it from the angle of murder as well."

—"By the way, the reason was not for even suicide. Why is this whitener being applied in the reports all over the place?"
Laxmikant pointed at the file.

—"Hey, it's normal here. There may have been some typing mistakes, which should have been rectified."

—"No...no, how can you do that? Will you do that? This is unacceptable being against rule. Anyone can manipulate with the whitener later. Also, every correction or change must be authenticated by signatures or initials."

Investigation by the CBI found that some manipulations have been done by the police in the case:-
In the investigation report, the injuries on Sister Mento's body were not taken seriously. In the case, physical evidence was destroyed such as the clothes of the deceased. From the file, photographs showing injuries on the body were removed.
The diary of the initial inquiry, which was written by ASI Inderjit, was also missing. The post-mortem report, chemical test and laboratory report were also modified by applying whitener from place to place. However, it was reported that in that region, it was common practice to ratify the reports by applying whitener.

CBI went to the church. Searched Sister Mento's room. Over there, things of general need were found.
CBI used the dummy and recreated the scene. A wax effigy was dragged from near the fridge and dropped

into the well. Scars were made on effigy, same as were on Sister Mento's body. From this, it was concluded that the possibility of murder cannot be ruled out. Someone must have hit Sister Mento on the head with a hammer, causing her to faint. Then the murderer must have dragged her to the well. Thereafter, the murderer must have thrown her in to the well. She must have died by drowning in the well in an unconscious state.

But the question was, who would have done this. There were guards outside and no one came at night. There was no enmity of her with anyone within the church. There was also no evidence of theft or rape. Two months passed. Even after the above analysis, the CBI could not make any arrests.

ASI Indrajit, lived alone in his flat. His mobile was not getting up. Later, the switch started coming off. After being absent from duty for two days, a man was sent from his office to see him at his home.

Neighbors told that Indrajit has not been seen outside the house for last two days. The guard of the society told that Indrajit used to go for jogging every morning, but he did not go for two days.

The cops reached Indrajit's flat. This time the media had also reached. The lock of the flat had been broken in the presence of the police. There was a slight bad smell inside. There was darkness in the room. A policeman lit the light. Indrajit's body was lying on the bed. A Glass having some liquid and some food items were lying nereby. Police said that Indrajit might have committed suicide by consuming poison. A suicide note was lying nearby. The media immediately took its photo and made it viral. In the suicide note, mental torture and pressure by senior officials of Inderjit and CBI was cited. The CBI had alleged that Inderjit destroyed the evidence and closed the case as a suicide, but the suicide note and the personal diary recovered from there showed that senior officers Hemant Pant and CBI in-charge Laxmikant had pressurized Inderjit. They destroyed the evidences gathered by ASI Indrajeet and accused him on the contrary.

The possibility was also written in the diary that Indrajit might be killed. Indrajit was getting a lot of threats to kill him continuously.

After that a lot of controversy arose. As a result, Laxmikant and Hemant Pant were removed from the case and investigation was set up against them. Laxmikant and Hemant Pant were suspended.

Now the case was handed over to CBI officers Saurabh Sanyasi and his in-charge Avadh Narayan. Both of them started the investigation of the case afresh. Now Indrajit's personal diary was an important evidence for this case.

In Indrajit's diary, suspicion was raised on three suspects - Pastor Williams, Pastor Victor and Nun Emilia. Because all three of them were present that night in that hostel building. Among them the brother of Pastor Victor was a man of political reach, and influencing the investigation. A church employee told Indrajit that Pastor Williams, Pastor Victor and Nun Emilia used to meet secretly and that something was going on between them. But the name of the employee was not recorded in the diary.

The police called all three for questioning. All three people were interrogated separately.

First, police officer called vector-
—"What was you doing that night?"

Vector replied-
—"I was in my room and was reading a religious book. Then I fell asleep."

the police asked again-
—"Did you hear any voice? Like... any squeak etc.?"

—"Nope."

—"About Sister Mento? Do you have any doubts?"

—"She was a simple lady. She used to work as a nurse in the hospital. That's all I know."

Then Williams and Emilia were called in turn. All three had almost the same answer.
All three were in their room that night and fell asleep while watching TV/books. Due to lack of evidence, the police could not arrest the three of them.

The matter reached to the court. The court had taken suo motu cognizance of the case due to public outrage. CBI was called. Pastor Williams, Pastor Victor and Nun Emilia were also summoned. But they did not reach the court. They were afraid of arrest. Their lawyer had arrived on their behalf.

The judge asked the CBI officer-
—"What is the progress in the Sister Mento murder case?"

CBI officer replied-
—"There is progress, but no conclusion has been arrived at. We have got a lot of help from ASI Inderjeet's diary. It suspects Pastor Williams, Pastor Victor and Nun Emilia, but no evidence has been found so far."

Court reprimands CBI and police for slow progress in the case-

—"Why the evidence has not been found yet. What are you doing? What is your plan for further investigation now?"

CBI officer sought permission-
—"We would like to have Pastor Williams, Pastor Victor and Nun Emilia undergo a narco test."

In narco polygraph test, the accused is injected with a drug, after which his reasoning power becomes weak for some time. In this situation he cannot tell a lie. His statement is taken after the injection. Although, it is sometimes not considered as part of humanity. This was strongly opposed by the counsel of Pastor Williams, Pastor Victor and Nun Emilia. But after some thought, the court ordered all three to undergo narco polygraph test.
Narco polygraph test was done on the orders of the court. The CD of the Narco Polygraph Test, presented in the court on the second day. But in the CD of the test, nothing special came to the light. The CD also reported the same thing that all three were in their rooms that night and had fallen asleep while watching TV or reading books.

Then suddenly the case took a new turn. CBI officer Saurabh Sanyasi resigned from the service of CBI. He called a press conference and announced that he had resigned from the CBI.
The journalist asked-
—"Sir, you were holding an important position in the CBI. Will you tell the public why you resigned?"

Saurabh replied-
—"While joining the CBI, I had taken an oath that I would do my work impartially, for justice. But actually, I am now fed up with unnecessary pressure."

Another journalist asked-
—"Who's putting pressure on you?"

Saurabh said-
—"Persons of political reach and also some senior officials."

According to Saurabh Sanyasi, his conscience did not allow him to follow the instruction given by his superior officer Mr. Awadh Narayan. He was pressurizing him to register the case as suicide and cover up the matter. With this press conference, the matter has, once again, attracted media attention. Another vigorous debate started on this matter.
Then, the media surrounded Awadh Narayan while coming out of his office. Journalists started asking him question on question-
—"Sir, your junior officer has accused you of pressurizing him for registering the case as a suicide and to cover up the matter. What do you have to say about this?"

At first Awadh Narayan tried a lot to avoid it, but then he had to say-
—"Look, if Saurabh had a complaint against me, he should have filed a complaint with an officer ranked above me. By unnecessarily leaking the matter of the case to the media, he has violated the rules of CBI. Action will be taken against him as per the rules."

Another journalist asked-
—"Who do you think, who is behind all this, who is putting pressure?"

Avadh Narayan now refused to answer-

—"No more question please. The investigation is going on. When something concrete comes out, you will be informed."

Then Avadh Narayan sat in his car. He closed the car door and also the window glass. Then he left from there.

Eventually Avadh Narayan was also dropped from the case. Now, Venkateswara, a retired judge, has been given the responsibility of the case.
Meanwhile, allegations of tampering with the narco test were made in the media. On the orders of the court, the CBI sent the CD to the forensic lab for examination. The forensic lab denied any manipulation in its report.
But an employee of that forensic lab, Lab Assistant Zoya, made a statement in the media that the test report was tampered with and she was receiving constant threats. She called a local news channel-
—"…Hello. The ruckus news channel?"

From there, came the voice-
— "Yes, I am speaking from the ruckus news channel, Chief Editor. Who are you?"

—"I am speaking from the forensic lab, lab assistant Zoya. You must have heard about the Sister Mento murder case. I have important information related to this case."

The curiosity of the chief editor of the ruckus news channel increased. After all, a loud news story was building up.
—"What is the information? Can you come and meet me at my office?"

—"No, my life is in danger. For the time being, you should know that the CD of Narco Test, which came to us for examination, was tampered with. The president of our lab changed the original report and gave a fake report that there was no manipulation."

Chief Editor asked-
—"How can I believe you? Do you have any proof? Hello? Hello, Miss Zoya, can you hear me?"

By then the phone was disconnected. The ruckus news channel tried to contact Zoya, which was unsuccessful. She was not even found at home. However, seeing no option, the ruckus news channel telecasted the recording of the conversation on TV.

Vikram was the president of the forensic lab. He was drinking tea sitting at home. The TV was on in front of him. He jumped on hearing the news. The next day, the police reached his house to interrogate him. But a different scene was there. At his home, Vikram had called a press conference. Lab President Vikram issued a statement to the press saying that Zoya was removed from the lab because she had presented a fake birth certificate at the time of appointment. That's why she was giving an ulterior statement to take revenge, and her statement should not be taken seriously.

Meanwhile, the original CD of the narco polygraph test got leaked on TV channel and YouTube. According to that leaked CD, the narco analysis investigation revealed that Sister Mento got up in the middle of the night, went down the stairs and went to the kitchen of the residence to drink water from the fridge.
Pastor Williams, Pastor Victor and Nun Emilia were having an ongoing relationship. They would often meet at night and quench their thirst in some hostel room. Since the new hostel building had been built and almost

all the staff had shifted there, there was total silence in that old building.

That night also, the three of them were on their way to a hostel room when Sister Mento saw them. All three went to the room and closed the door of the room from inside. Out of curiosity, Sister Mento peeped through the keyhole and found all three in a objectionable position. But suddenly Sister Mento's mobile rang. Sister Mento ran away in panic.

Victor was shocked to hear the sound of the mobile. He told William and Emilia-
—"It seems someone has seen us, it was the sound of her mobile."

All three were terrified. If the relations between the three had been revealed, not only they would have to face embarrassment but would also be thrown out of the church. All of three immediately left the room. They ran and caught Sister Mento. Before she could scream, Victor put a cloth over her mouth, so that her voice was buried in her throat. Emilia striked her from behind with an axe, causing Sister Mento to fall. Then the killers hit her on the head again, due to which she fainted. Then, thinking that she was dead, the three murderers dragged her away and threw her into the well behind the building.

The court immediately swung into action as soon as the CD was leaked. Immediately directed to get the CD tested outside the state. The investigation found that the CD had been manipulated at 30 places.

Now the lab president Vikram has been arrested for tampering with the evidence. The police interrogated him strictly-
—"Tell me, what manipulations have you done on the CD?"

Vikram replied-
—"Actually, CD was manipulated at 30 places to make fake CD. The original CD contained the confessions of the criminals."

The police officer gave him two slaps in anger. Then asked-
—"Tell, at whose behest did you tamper with the CD?"

Vikram panicked. He started joining hands and feet. spoke-
—"If I take their name, they will kill me. Save me, I don't want to die."

On being given a lot of assurances from the police, Vikram told the name of an important politician who has asked him to do so.

The police again asked-
—"Why did you do this, how much money did you take?"

Vikram told-
—"I had taken one crore rupees for this."

On his spotting, the bribe money was also recovered. Simultaneously, Pastor Williams, Pastor Victor and Nun Emilia were arrested for the murder of Sister Mento.

Now, the matter was in court. Amelia was standing in the dock of courtroom. The public prosecutor asked-
—"Miss Emilia, do you confess to your crime?"

Emilia flatly refused-
—"No, I have never had a relationship with Williams nor with Victor. I am completely virgin. All the allegations leveled against me are false."

The public prosecutor laughed, said-
—"Whom are you deceiving? It has been proved in the narco test that you had relations with both Williams and Victor..."

Lawyer in defence objected-
—"Objection My lord, by law, narco tests are treated as clues and are not concrete evidence. I am presenting this virginity certificate to substantiate the statement made by Emilia in the court. You can get it confirmed at your level."

The judge adjourned the case for a week, ordering Emilia's virginity test to be conducted by an independent medical officer.
First, the CBI entrusted a local doctor on its panel to conduct a medical examination of Emilia. On medical examination, she was proved to be a virgin, which weakened the case as the court considers the narco test as clue and not concrete evidence.
Considering the tampering of evidence done by the accused earlier, now the CBI has got Emilia tested for virginity in a high capacity medical lab. This time the CBI was trying not to let any mistake happen, they have already been accused of negligence. This time CBI got success. This test proved that Emilia was a virgin, but she had herself operated on to make it look like this. She got that operation done by a foreign doctor. The operation was carried out so meticulously, that even the local CBI doctor, who had conducted the medical examination of Emilia, was dodged.
Now all the paths of the criminals were closed. All three criminals confessed to the crime. On their confession, the police, CBI and people of various institutions were arrested, who were responsible for breaking the case and tampering with the evidence. Victor's brother, a

politician, was also arrested for misleading the court and criminal conspiracy.

But this case proves that some times media and courts do their work more credibly. And the criminal can distort his case in any way, if he has money and political access.

CHAPTER 4
GANGSTER WIFE

The "Famous Restaurant" was a well-known and very expensive restaurant in the city. The three-storey building, parking in the basement and the bar, used to be visited only by the prominent people of the city.

On the evening of 7th May, an expensive red colored car stopped there. Out of that, Vinita and her husband Robert descended. Robert was a well-known actor while his wife Vinita was also a successful actress. Today, Robert was driving the car himself. He gave the car keys to the concierge, and asked him to put the car in the parking lot. The concierge took the car to park it in the basement.

Vinita was the second wife of actor Robert. His first wife had died. That day, Vinita went to have dinner with Robert at the famous restaurant.

Robert was in a suit as usual. Along with this, his licensed pistol was also hanging from the waist. Vinita was wearing a mini skirt that day and was looking gorgeous. Both sat in the cabin inside the restaurant. There was solitude.

The waiter put the menu card on the table, along with two glasses and a bottle of water. Robert picked up the menu card. Looked for a while, then extended towards Vinita. He spoke-

—"Look, what do you like to order?"

Vinita started looking at the menu. Meanwhile, the concierge had put the keys of the car on the table, after parking the car in the parking lot.

Both ordered food and wine of their choice.

Vinita was eating fast, as if she was in a hurry. At the same time, Robert was immersed in some thought. There was a lack of dialogue between the two. Seeing him immersed in thought, Vinita said-

Nidhi Gupta

—"What's the matter, Robert, you haven't even finished your soup yet?"

Robert awake from his thinking. He replied-
—"Am, oh yes, I was thinking of something."

Vinita asked-
—"Anything to worry about?"

Robert assured her-
—"Oh no, just some business issues. Well, tell me, something else will you take?"

Vinita replied-
—"No, I've already finished my meal."

After the meal, they started going back. Robert and Vinita reached the basement. Robert was about to start the car when he remembered that his licensed firearm had been left behind in the restaurant. Robert said-
—"Oh my god, I forgot my gun on the table. Darling, you get in the car. I'll just bring the gun. Take this key, you may start the AC."

Robert went back to get the gun. Vinita opened the door of the car and sat on the driver's seat. She started the engine, then she started the AC.
Vinita was sitting in the car parked in that parking area. Then came the sound of firing bullets. An unknown gunman shot five bullets and killed Vinita. After firing, the gunman fled from the spot.
Robert heard the sound of bullets. He came running. The window of the car was completely broken. He opened the car door. Vinita's body rolled out. There were bullets in the head and chest. He took the body back and put it inside the car. Seeing the dead body,

Robert started sobbing. The restaurant owners informed the police.

Police came. The policemen got done Panchnama (Paperwork) of the body and sent it for postmortem. The firing of five bullets indicated that the attack was actually done for the purpose of killing. All of Five bullets had hit Vinita. Not a single one here and there. The precise firing of the bullets indicated that the killer must have been a professional killer.

The post-mortem report came the next day. The cause of death in the report was given as severe damage to vital organs due to bullets and bleeding. The policemen started the investigation. From the neighborhood, it came to know that the relationship between Robert and Vinita was not going well and there was a situation of divorce. Even Vinita's children had confirmed this. The policemen first called Robert for questioning, then arrested him.

There was also a reason for suspicion, that that Robert had escaped thereby making Vinita sit in the car, pretending to take his gun. The matter went to court.

Robert was charged with murder and conspiracy to murder Vinita. But the court not found Robert guilty of the offenses due to lack of evidence and released him.

About seven months later, the case against Robert was reopened by Vinita's children.

During the investigation, it came to know that Vinita was an ambitious woman from her teenage. Her parents were from a middle class family. Vinita did not feel like studying and writing. Her mother was worried, she would often explain to her-

—"Daughter, put your mind to studies. We have high hopes from you. We have no son. If you could become something by studying..."

But Vinita replied-

—"Oh mother, what to do after studying and writing, job like father? I will be a model."
She had the ghost of becoming a model in her brain.

Mother said again-
—"Daughter, dreaming is a good thing, but one should keep one's feet on the ground of reality."

Vinita said-
—"I have so many dreams, I will be a very successful model one day. Mother, you will see, I will have a lot of name, money, Big Bunglow and car. Everything will be available to us."

Vinita dropped out of studying after completing her high school at the age of 16. And she decided to move to the city of Washington to pursue a career in modeling. She started getting work there, with her beautiful body. But she was getting less money for her work, due to being new comer. And above all, the big expenses of a big city of Washington. But after striving a lot, she abled to took a rented flat and a second hand car.
One day she was going in her car. On the way her car got stopped suddenly. Despite several attempts, it did not turn on. It was evening. Vinita got very upset. She opened the bonnet of the car. But she could not understand anything. Then suddenly, a voice came from her behind-
—"Hello ma'am, what can I help you with?"

Vinita looked back. A man standing, with a French cut beard. He was wearing a round hat. He had worn shirt with flowers & leaves and trousers. There was a touch of French in his voice.

He chuckled. Spoke-
—"I am Sam. Sam DiCosta. I think you're in trouble."

Vinita told her problem to him. DiCosta checked the car. Then made his face bad and said -
—"Its radiator has burst. A mechanic will have to be called to make it."

Concern appeared on Vinita's face. she said-
—"Oh, what will happen now?"

Sam offered-
—"If you agree, I can drop you off to your house. You later, send the mechanic and get the car brought."

—"Okay."
Vinita heaved a sigh of relief and agreed.

He was a French citizen DiCosta, who was an immigrant. He needed to be married to live in the United States. After then, the two started dating. DiCosta told Vinita his desire to settle in America. If he married an American woman, he could get US citizenship. He was even ready to pay a considerable amount for this.
Vinita married him for the sake of money from him. But later, DiCosta could not pay the full amount. On not getting the full amount, Vinita broke the marriage and got divorced from him. There was no physical relationship between the two. In the absence of any child, DiCosta was exiled.

Later due to financial constraints, Vinita started doing erotic photo shoots. She used to dance in private parties and earn money. Eventually Vinita was able to buy a flat in Los Angeles. Bad habits came as soon as money came. Along with alcohol, she also started taking drugs. Her indecent photos and dance videos went viral on the internet.

At the age of 21, Vinita married a 44-year-old man named Pental. This was Pental's second marriage. Vinita and Pental had two children, Gerry and Harry. But this relationship did not last long. The reason was Vinita's openness. Also, Vinita soon realized that she had made a mistake by marrying a man much older than her. Vinita's age was frivolous, while Pental's nature was serious due to elderly age. Neither he was able to give her happiness of being husband properly, nor was he interested in so much touring. Both of them started quarreling every day. Pental expounded to her-
—"Vinita, I have told you many times to give up the habit of roaming here and there. We have two children. You always leave them alone at home and go to have fun."

Vinita replied-
—"Pental, you are old, now fun is not just about you. I'm still young, I have some dreams, aspirations."

Pental insisted-
—"In the pursuit of your desires, my home and family will be destroyed. How will your children think about your coming home after drinking every day? Do I not know, what adultery do you made with your friends."

Bringing hatred in her voice, Vinita said-
—"Your thinking is very conservative."
Due to the lack of views of the two, the rift between them was increasing on a daily basis, and after five or six years of marriage, they got divorced.

Vinita had a history of befriending celebrities. Her friends and relatives told the police during interrogation that she was very famous among celebrities due to her attractive personality.
One day, Vinita went to an opera club. There she had a dance program. It was evening. There were many

guests in the club. Vinita was wearing a black dress that day, which was giving more beauty to her fair body. She danced wonderfully. Her show was followed by program of an opera singer named Monty.

After her program, Vinita started drinking alcohol in the same bar. After a while Monty's performance also ended. After that he also came to the bar. Monty started drinking while sitting on the seat next to Vinita. The two started talking.

Monty said-

—"You did a great dance."

Vinita laughed and replied-

—"Thank you, your opera singing was prodigious too."

It was night after drinking. Both drank a lot. That night, Vinita had drunk too much in the conversation, she rolled over. Monty dropped Vinita to her house.

For the next several days, they both had their programs there. One day, it went a long night while eating together and drinking alcohol. After this Monty went to drop Vinita at her house. But that night Monty also had drunk too much. They both got drunk.

—"..... I find you very beautiful Vinita, I think I have started falling in love with you."

Monty said taking Vinita in his arms. But then Monty felt that he was doing something wrong. He pulled his hands back.

Vinita grabbed his hand and placed it on her shoulders and said-

—"Oh Monty, you have spoken to my heart. I can't live without you either."

Both of them got embraced. Then kissed together.

Then, both of them stayed together all night and quenched their thirst. After that both of them continued to meet. The two also started doing programs together.
In this sequence, Vinita started live-in relationship with opera singer Monty. After about a year and a half, Vinita gave birth to a baby girl. At first, Monty was very happy and surprised too. Surprised because he was told by the doctors that because of a childhood accident, he could never become a father. On arising suspicion, he got the DNA tested of baby girl and it was proved that the daughter was not of Monty. His heart was broken by Vinita's infidelity. Both got separated.

Vinita named the daughter as Mary. but Vinita was getting very upset. Her daily schedule was finding it difficult to be managed because of her baby girl. One day, she thought something in herself and called her ex-husband, Pental over telephone. She said -
—"Hello Pental, I want to meet you."

Pental was surprised by her sudden call. Spoke-
—"How did you think of here today, sweetheart?"

In response Vinita said-
—"I'll tell you when we meet."

Pental said-
—"Come on, I'm at home."

Vinita reached Pental's house. Pental was at home. Both the children had gone to school. When Pental saw her, he asked-
—"Vinnie, how are you?"

Pental used to call her by this name. Vinita smiled in reply-
—"I am Okay, tell me of yours."

Pental laughed faintly. Then said-
—"Look, I am in front of you. But business is going a bit slow."

Vinita said being serious-
—"I can do something, if you want."

At the moment, Pental's attention shifted to the girl mary. Vinita had taken her daughter with herself. Pental asked-
—"Who is this girl?"

Vinita said-
—"This is me and my second, I mean…the third husband's child. But we are divorced."

Pental expressed fake regret-
—"Oh, I'm sorry."

—"But I am not. I have an offer for you. If you keep this girl with you and take care of her, then I am ready to pay you monthly money."

Pental business was not going well. Vinita left her Daughter Mary with her ex-husband Pental, with the condition that she would provide him expenses and financial support. Pental was in hard time, he got ready.

One day Vinita was going to her flat and was drunk. After Vinita's vulgar photos and dance videos went viral on the internet, she became quite infamous. The lift guard made some explicit remarks on Vinita, on which she lost her control and started fighting with him. The lift guard called the police. Seeing the police, Vinita got furious and started taking off her clothes and threatened

to sue the policemen for sexual harassment. The policemen got panicked and called the lady police.
Vinita was arrested by the police, for drug consuming, nature of her business and other behaviors. Later, she was jailed for 6 months.
When Vinita was sent to jail on drug charges, she met a gangster named Dawood, who was also in jail. Vinita was locked in the women's cell, Dawood was in the men's cell. But at the time of eating, the inmates of both the cells were served food together. Dawood used to use his influence to eat good food even in jail. Seeing Vinita, he was floored. Vineeta was also surprised to see Dawood's prestige and pride.
The two met during dinner. Vinita was asking for an extra piece of meat from the prison staff, while the jail staff was serving food according to the jail manual. Arguments started between the two.

Dawood stood there, watching the two quarreling. He reached the food counter, then he intervened-
—"Don't worry, Lady Don, I will show you how to get your rights."

He hurriedly picked up two pieces of meat and put them on Vinita's plate. The prison staff was aware of Dawood's influence. He could not speak out of fear.
Then Vinita was invited by Dawood to have dinner with him. Vinita came to Dawood's table with her plate. A conversation started between the two. Dawood asked-
—"Which crime did you get involved for jail?"

—"For the offense of taking drugs. and you?"

—"If there is just one crime, then I might tell you. There are many charges against me."

At first the two started eating together. Then in the night, after giving money to the jail guard, the two also started meeting. Vinita had started a physical relationship with Dawood. One night Vinita was there with Dawood in his cell. That cell was in the corner, in front of the cell was the gallery, followed by the wall. She said-
—"Dawood, I'm afraid, what if any prison worker comes to this side?"

—"Nothing, I have paid a lot of money to the guard of the gallery here. He is my own man."

—"But in this cell everything is open. I feel awkward and feeling shyness."

Dawood assured her-
—"It may be open here, but there is a wall in front, and in this gallery, no one can come here being that guard there."

Finally Vineeta agreed. And the nights of both started getting colorful everyday.

Time passed and Dawood came out after serving his jail sentence, and Vinita also came out freed from drug charges. But their relationship continued outside the jail as well.
Using Dawood's good influence, Vinita started working in movies. On the movies shooting set, she met Robert, an out-of-touch actor. But here, Vinita did a double cross and had started an affair with Robert as well. However, Robert was aware of her prior relationship with Dawood. Vinita again became pregnant and gave birth to a son, whom she named Amin. This is because Vinita thought that the father of the child was Dawood. Then later, Vinita told Robert that she was unsure of the child's paternity, and that Robert was probably the child's

father. After DNA testing it was determined that Robert was the actual father of the child. After paternity was established, the child was legally named as "Wight".
With this, for the good future of the child, both of them started agreeing for the marriage. But Vinita put a condition. Under the condition, if the husband decides to end the marriage, Vinita will keep the child with her, and Robert will have to bear the costs and damages of both her and the child. Whereas nothing like this happens in divorce by wife.

Robert was surprised to hear the condition. He said-
—"What is this Vinita, don't you have trust on me? We are going to tie in the bond of marriage."

Vinita insisted-
—"Sorry Robert, but in this short life, I have seen many ups and downs. I don't want that our relationship too have a bad ending and it will affect our child."

Robert still didn't understand anything-
—"I do not understand whether this is happening a marriage or a contract?"

Vinita stood firm on her decision and said-
—"If there will be marriage between us, then only after the signing of the agreement, otherwise not."

Eager to marry with Vinita, Robert accepted the condition and he had to sign the agreement. Then, he married with Vinita.
Even after the marriage, Vinita did not deter herself from her antics. Her all-night parties and dating with other men were continued. But after a year, Robert started feeling bad about Vinita's going on dates with other men. An altercation started between the two.
One day they had a big fight. Robert said angrily-

—"Vinita, you are going out of bounds. I don't like you dating with other men at all."

Vinita explained to him-
—"Robert, you are an actor yourself, you know how important it is to attend parties in this field."

Robert objected-
—"Yes, I know, but attending parties is one thing. And doing immorality under the guise of parties is another."

Vinita said intensifying her voice-
—"Your thinking is very bad. How can you even think of me like that? I also know all about, where your affairs are going on."

The next morning, at breakfast, Robert was staring at his son. His mood was disturbed with the fight that took place last night. Then not knowing what came in his mind that he took his son and went to the doctor in the car. There, he gave his son's and his own blood for a DNA testing. The report came the next day. His suspicion was correct, wight was not his son.

Robert was now aware of Vinita's infidelity. He hired a private detective to spy behind her. He started thinking of getting divorced from her, but he was trapped under the agreement. If he gives divorce to Vinita by himself, he had to pay a hefty amount to Vinita as compensation. He also came to know that the report of the DNA test report produced by Vinita to prove paternity of Wight, was false. Wight was not his son, but Vinita had lied to him.

During the investigation, the police thought that in order to get rid of Vinita due to above reason, Robert must have killed her. In case of death, he does not have to pay any compensation to the wife. In fact, he had gone to the restaurant to get his gun, which he had brought for his self-defense, as he was receiving threats. The opinion of the police was that Robert had got Vinita killed by hiring a professional killer.

While Robert maintained that he had sufficient evidence that Vinita was unfaithful and that Wight was not his son, he would not have to pay any damages, and on that basis he was considering to apply for divorce.

The investigation also raised the possibility that Vinita was murdered by one of the men whom Vinita was blackmailing. Because the police had recovered objectionable photographs of many people from Vinita's flat. The police believed that Vinita was using those photographs to blackmail some people.

Nothing was recovered from the site of the incident, i.e. the basement of the hotel, except a few empty cases of rounds of bullets.

The private detective, who followed Vinita, told the police that Vinita had been in contact with Dawood even after her marriage with Robert. The police also decided to see it from Dawood's angle now.

The information of Dawood's henchmen was received by the informer. Dawood's mobile was put on tapping.

A lot came out of the telephonic conversation between Vinita's children and Dawood. Dawood was advising Vinita's children on how to capture the property by implicating Robert in the murder case. For this, the lawyer was also provided by the Dawood. Now, it was decided to interrogate Dawood. Dawood, who was out of jail on parole, on the pretext of illness, was arrested. Upon rigorous interrogation, the whole thing came to the fore. Dawood confessed to give Vinita a professional killer to kill the Robert. The professional killer was also arrested on his trail.

Vinita had, in fact, learned that Robert came to know that Wight was not his son. Because of this, Robert was about to divorce Vinita. Wight was actually Dawood's son. Vinita went for legal advice.

She went to her lawyer Mr. Nixon. She reminded him about the agreement executed at the time of marriage. She said-
—"Mr. Nixon, do you remember, at the time of my marriage, you got my husband to sign the agreement. Subject to the condition of the agreement, if my husband decides to end the marriage, I will keep the child with me, and Robert will bear the costs and damages of both mine and the child."

Mr. Nixon nodded as yes.

Vinita further said-
—"Now my husband wants to divorce me."

Mr. Nixon assured her-
—"No problem. We have an agreement signed by your husband. If he divorces you, he will have to pay expenses and damages."

But Vinita's concern was another. She said-
—"Mr. Nixon, my husband finds out that Wight is not, in fact, his son."

Now, Mr. Nixon also getting worried, said-
—"Oh my god! It got so bad."

The lawyer advises her that if Robert divorces her on the grounds of infidelity and adultery, she will not be able to get any amount from him. Vinita got very worried and upset after hearing this.
For this, Vinita went to Dawood. She told him everything and asked for help.
Dawood, not taking interest in her case, said-
—"Vinita, the problem with you is that, you haven't been loyal to anyone. Why should I help you?"
There was indifference in Dawood's voice.

Vinita tried to explain him-
—"Dawood, it is not that I have done anything hiding with you. Also, Wight is your own son. I had some dreams. I did what I could do to accomplish them. Dawood, I have achieved this position with a lot of hard work. I don't want to lose them all. I want to come back to you. I promise that I will always be yours."

Dawood suggested-
 "There is only one cure for all this. That is your husband's death. I will kill your husband."
It was in Dawood's mind that if Robert was killed, he could inherit both Vinita and her husband's property also.

Vinita was surprised and said-
—".....What?"
Vinita got very scared. She didn't want to get into all these troubles. But now she had no choice.
Ultimately, Vinita agreed with Dawood to get Robert killed. In the event of Robert's death, being the wife, Vinita would get all the properties and money Robert had.
For this, Dawood gave her his trusted killer. According to the plan, the killer was to hit Robert, while he would be in the car, at the parking lot in the basement of the restaurant. But the killer did not know that Vinita had also gone along with him in the car. With the black film attached to glasses of windshield of the car, he could not recognize Vinita and fired five shots from a distance, so that Robert could not escape. Vinita got hit by all the bullets and she herself collapsed.
Later, Vinita's children sued Robert so that Robert could be hanged to death or sentenced a long term jail and Dawood's son, Wight, could become the owner of the property. Behind all this, there was Dawood. He was

constantly providing them with instructions and legal facilities. But his attempt could not be successful. Robert was acquitted. Dawood and his gang were arrested and sent to jail for conspiracy to murder and murder.

Vinita had to face the consequences for her knavery. She got caught in her own trap and had to die.

CHAPTER 5
TO REGRET

Kashmir is truly a heaven on the earth. Apples and nuts orchards, saffron beds. Neatly planted pine and devdaar trees. Snow falling lightly on them.

Along with Dal Lake, surrounded by a boulevard, adorned with gardens, parks, houseboats and hotels of the Mughal era. Shikaras hovering in the water of the lake. During the winter season, sometimes the temperature would drop too low and the lake water would freeze.

Ahmed was a 12-year-old teenager. He was studying in a government school there. His mother, father and younger sister Rukhsana were in his house. His father had a small business. There was financial constraint in the family. They lived in a small house in the Kashmir Valley.

It was eight in the morning. Outside, it was sunny today. In the room of the house, Ahmed was lying on the cot with his eyes closed. His mother was preparing food. Ahmed's school was from nine AM in the morning. His mother came to his bed to see him. She was surprised to see him sleeping. Said-
—"Hey, this boy is still asleep."

Then she started shaking him.
—"Ahmed, Ahmed!"

Ahmed was sleeping. He said in a lazy voice-
—"…..Um... don't….. mommy, let me sleep."
His mother nodded-

—"Get up. Go to the bathroom and take a bath and get ready immediately. It's time to go to school. You will be late."

Ahmed got up with drowsiness in his eyes, took the towel and entered in the bathroom. Then came out after taking a bath. Then asked his mother-
—" Mom, what's in the food?"

Mother replied-
—"Bread and lentils with hawk leaves."

Ahmed was watching. His mother was making a splash by putting hawk leaves in the pan. Then poured cooked lentils in it and covered it with the pan.
A nice aroma was coming out of the kitchen, reaching Ahmed's nose.

Ahmed got ready wearing his school uniform. He said to mother-
 —" Mommy, I'm ready, please comb my hair."

His mother brought a comb. She combed his hair.

Then Ahmed's eyes fell on his younger sister Rukhsana. She was sleeping soundly. Ahmed said-
—"Mommy, why don't you pick up this witch early in the morning?"

Then he went to Rukhsana to wake her up. On her face, Ahmed applied cold water held in his hand. Rukhsana started murmuring.

Mother forbade him-
—"Let her stay, Ahmed, don't pick her up. Moreover, her school is by 12 o'clock, if she wakes up now, she will bother me unnecessarily."

Boys' school used to start from nine o'clock in the morning, while that of girls from twelve o'clock.

After eating breakfast, Ahmed went to school. As he went to school, his mother took care of the household chores. Then she readied Rukhsana for school and sent her to the school.

Then she started weaving mats. She learned this art in a handicraft program of an NGO. This would have given her some extra income to help her in running household.

Ahmed loved his sister very much. Whenever he had money, he would bring something for her. Sometimes toffies, sometimes ribbons or marbles.

On his way back that day, Ahmed had brought toffies for his sister. He went to her and said-
—"Look, what I brought for you."

Rukhsana was very happy to see the toffies –
—"Wow, Toffee, brother you are so good."

Ahmed himself was very happy seeing her happiness. In this way the days were passing happily. Despite the lack of money in the house, there was a hope that Ahmed would hold great position a day, by his study and would bring his parents and family out of poverty, bringing glory to everyone.

One day Ahmed was coming back from his school. It was not sunny today. There was a cool breeze all over. Ahmed's feet were moving fast on the unpaved trail. Got hungry. Perhaps, Ammi must have prepared something good today, to eat.

Then on the way some boys called him-
—"Ahmed, Ahmed!"

Ahmed looked astonished. Then asked-
—"What is it?"

They called him-
—"Will you go with us to drink kahwa on the banks of the dal lake."

Ahmed refused-
—"I will not. Mommy has forbidden me to go anywhere and asked me to come straight home from school."

Bad wind was blowing in those days. At the age of studying ABC, boys were tricked in the name of Kashmir and religion and sent to camps across the border.
Ahmed refused and got on his way. Those boys also went their own way.

It went on like this for many days, one day again, those boys met him.

This time they had Rupees in their hands. Waving the note, they said-
—"Come on, Let's go to listen the speech of "Saheb. Fifty rupees will be given to you."
Saheb was their leader who used to get people gathered by giving money.

Ahmed looked at the note in surprise-
—"Fifty rupees?"
This time Ahmed's eyes lit up. What would he buy with fifty rupees, he began to calculate.
But mommy has forbidden him, well, seeing the money, maybe, she will scold him a less. Anyway, for fifty rupees he would have agreed to get beaten.

And he calculating all the accounts, went with them. It was an open field. The bearded "saheb" was giving a speech sitting there on the chair. Many people were listening to the speech sitting on the carpet at the ground. He told about the problems of the people of Kashmir. Told some facts about religious things too. Then cursed India wholeheartedly. Told Pakistan as his mentor.

Then Ahmad was sent to the congregation of big leaders.
For a few days, Ahmed listened to the speeches of leaders who were taught their own children abroad. And their children were either in good jobs or doing profitable business. But they were engaged in making frenzy by instigating other's children.
They used to get a lot of money from Pakistan for this, due to which those people had built up their properties in India and abroad.

Slowly Ahmed's mindset started changing. Seeing the soldiers earlier, he felt a sense of security. But now seeing the army men, his blood would boil.

And one day...
Ahmed went missing. It was heard that he went to Pakistan for training with the terrorists. God knows, whether he went on his own volition or by forceful abduction.
Ahmed was blindfolded. He and a few other boys were taken sometimes by car and sometimes on foot.
On the way, it became night. They stopped for food and water. It was an unknown place. The blindfold was opened. Food and water were given. It was a cold night, a boy tried to light a fire.
A man slapped him hard from behind. The boy fell. The man shouted-

—"How will you light a fire here? I mean do you know? Seeing the smoke, the soldiers will find us."

The boy stood up, rubbing his cheek.
Ahmed was terrified. His heart wanted him to run away, to his mother and father. But his leader threatened all those boys that if anyone ran back from there, the whole family including his parents, siblings would be killed.
Then, they were made to cross the canal by boat at night. In the night, Pakistan fired heavily along the Line of Control. Under its cover, they entered Pakistan-occupied Kashmir.
On the other hand, Ahmed's mother and father cried a lot. Rukhsana was also very Sad and crying continuously. A lot of search was done by police, but nothing was found. But at the end, when the tracer was not found, the files of missing Report were covered with a layer of dust over time.
There, Ahmed was first taken to a terrorist training camp in Pakistan.
A masked person made everyone sit and interviewed. Then everyone was brainwashed with books, videos and speeches for several days. Then with the right-wrong logic, poison was filled in their mind against India and other religions.
Then from the next day onwards, their rigorous training was started. They were trained to operate AK-47 and other fatal weapons. Then they were taught to throw bombs.
At night there was turmoil in Ahmed's mind. He would remember his home, feeling that he was doing something wrong. One day he decided to talk to his trainer about this.
Ahmed asked fearfully-
 —"How can we kill someone, that would be a crime."

The trainer replied-

—"Killing the infidels, raping their women, is an act of great pride. Kill them, rob them, set their houses on fire. Even if you become a martyr in this path, then seventy two elves will worship you at the door of paradise."

Then after being silent for a while, the trainer again said-
—"At the same time, we have to destroy those Indian Muslims also."

Ahmed was surprised-
—"Why, they are our own brother. What crime have they committed?"

The trainer cried out in anger-
—"Their fault is that they are Indians, and India is our enemy country."

Every kind of poison was sown in Ahmed's mind. Also, rigorous military training was given. As a result, after eight years, he was now a staunch terrorist. For him now, every Indian was his enemy, irrespective of religion.
Ahmed had now forgotten his family. However, some hazy memories were still in his mind.

A few days later, he was sent to the border areas of Afghanistan to do experimental examples.
Those people made their base there in the hills of Hindukush. There, a construction company got the contract to build a bridge nearby.
The terrorists sent a letter to that company and demanded an amount of one lakh dollars. Threats were made, to stop the work and kill the workers, if the money was not received.

On receiving the letter, the in-charge got very upset. He informed the director of his company. The director informed the police there. Seeing the seriousness of the matter, the police deployed four policemen.

At this Ahmed and his companions became very angry. After this, many times the terrorists threatened to send recovery or stop the work to that company, but the money did not reach. The Company was sure due to deployment of the policemen.

An Afghan engineer was also working there in that bridge constructing company. One day when he was returning home from office in his car, terrorists were ambushed him on the way. A man stood in front of the car with a gun pointed at him.

The Afghan engineer saw the gunman. He felt some danger. He drove his car from the side and took it. But that gunman shot at the tyres of his car. Suddenly the car overturned due to tyre burst.

The terrorists took him out of the car, then made some speeches while making videos. Then, Ahmed killed the Afghan engineer.

The video was released through the Internet and other mediums. An atmosphere of fear was created there. Now whenever they sent letters, money would start coming in.

This was the first murder for Ahmed. But after that, the cycle started.

Later, Ahmed was posted in Balochistan by the ISI. Balochistan was forcibly occupied by Pakistan, which was opposed by its residents and leaders. Pakistan was digging minerals there with the help of China.

The local leader, Gafoor, was strongly opposing this. A large number of people gathered to listen his speech. His speeches were related to the suffering and pain of the common people of there.

That day also, Gafoor was giving a speech. A large crowd had gathered to hear his speech. Gafoor was speaking on the microphone-

—"Pakistan has illegally occupied our Balochistan. In our Balochistan, there is a lot of mineral and precious resources with grace of God. But we remain beggars. Why? Because we are not able to use our resources for our own. The government of Pakistan is using them. They are exploiting us by extracting our minerals through their companies. And what did the residents of here get in return? Nothing has been done for development of Balochistan. Not only this, these people without asking us, without taking our opinion, they gave the project to the Chinese company. Due to this we have had to leave our homes in large numbers and get displaced…."

There were two ISI agents in the crowd, who were recording his words. They went to their boss. They told the boss about Gafoor-
—"Sir, this Gafoor is again provoking the Balochistanis."

After listening to the recording, the boss asked-
—"How many people were there?"

Agents told-
—"That's about a thousand."

Boss got worried-
—"This Gafoor, may not get started riots somewhere. Project work will be stopped. Kill him."

The task of killing Gafoor was given to Ahmed and his associates.

The next morning some people reached outside Gafoor's house. They knocked at the door of his house, then called-
—"Gafoor Miyan, just come out, have to do some chatting."

Gafoor came out, saw that some people were standing there covered in blankets. They have hidden their faces with masks.
He asked in surprise-
—"What is it?"

One man said-
—"Come with us."

Gafoor got some apprehensive.
—"Who are you guys and where do you want to take me?"

Gafoor felt threatened. With suspicion of something wrong, Gafoor turned back. He was about to enter in the house, when Ahmed pointed a pistol on his forehead. Then took his mouth near gafoor's ear and whispered-
—"Gafoor Mian, if you do not want bloodshed, then sit quietly in the car. Otherwise, your family will be destroyed along with you. The rest, you yourself are smart."

Gafoor panicked and said-
—"No... No, I am ready to go with you. Don't do anything to my family."

Gafoor went and sat with them in the car. His eyes were blindfolded. Where did they take him, no one knew.
Nothing was known of Gafoor for a few days. Gafoor's family members got tired of persuading the police. Then after many days the mutilated body of Gafoor was found. Seeing the condition of the corpse, it could be assessed that Ahmed and his associates had tortured Gafoor a lot and then killed him.

Now Ahmed was desperate to wreak havoc in the Indian area. Then one day his head, whom they all called Aaka, called him.
Aaka said-
—"Today you are being sent on a mission…."

Ahmed asked curiously-
—"where?"

Aaka smiled-
—"I have come to know that you want to go on a mission in Kashmir. This time you are being sent there."

Ahmed's eyes gleamed with joy. He asked-
—"Aaka, what I have to do?"

Aaka told-
—"You raid in Kashmir, harass Kashmiris all by killing, raping, arson. We will put the blame on the Indian Army. There will be riots. Ha…ha…ha…."

Ahmed and his 4 companions went. They put on the clothes of the local shepherds. It was a cold night. Suddenly it started snowing. It was good for them. The army could not see anything in the snow, nor could they hear any sound.
The Pakistani army also started firing. The Indian army got busy in answering them. Taking advantage of the opportunity, Ahmed and his associates cut the barbed wire fence on the Line of Control, and entered in India.
After entering, they reached to the local agent. They had dinner there and spent the whole night. The local agent provided weapons to them and also gave some money.

Ahmed and his companions dressed themselves as local shepherds and kept some goats. During the day they would do spying while grazing goats, but at night they would come back in their original form. For many days, they roamed around, plundering and killing according to the orders of their master. If any girl ever got caught in their hands, then their night would also be arranged. After fulfilling their lust, they would put her to death too.

Ahmed was no longer the Ahmed who studied in the school. Who used to bring toffees for his sister. Who wanted to brighten the name of his parents by removing their poverty. Ahmed had now become a terrorist. He could kill anyone at the behest of his masters from across the border, whether one be innocent, old, child, woman, anyone. While raping the girls, he could no longer even remember that he ever had a sister. He had to fulfill the purpose of his master now, and only.

Criminal incidents had been increased. Police and army started investigation. The blockade was done and check posts were created. One day, while passing through a street, a soldier saw them. The soldier got suspicion over them. The soldier interrogated them-
—"Who are you guys? It doesn't seem you are local. Come on, show ID."

A colleague of Ahmed replied-
—"We are the poor shepherds. Our goats went somewhere. We are searching them"

The soldier was still suspicious. He said-
—"Let me search."

Then, suddenly Ahmed opened fire with his rifle and killed the soldier.
A colleague of Ahmed scolded him-
—"Why did you shoot now, if the soldiers came here after hearing the sound..."

His guess was right. The soldiers were arrived, but Ahmed and his companions managed to escape, taking advantage of the narrow galleries. The search had been started after the death of the soldier. Ahmed did not consider it appropriate to visit the agent's hideout. They knocked at the door of a house nearby.
The owner of the house asked-
—"who...who is it?...who is....?"

Not getting any response, the owner of the house curiously opened the door and started looking outside.
Ahmed and his companions were standing outside. One of companion of Ahmed said-
—"We are passengers, we want to spend the night at your house."

The owner of the house refused-
—"No, look elsewhere. There is no room in my house."

He happened to close the door, but then Ahmed, along with his companions, entered the house forcibly.

Ahmed removed his blanket and took the gun off his shoulder. Pointed the rifle at the old man, and said-
—"Listen old man, if you don't let us spend the night here, we will shot you."

Just then a gentle feminine voice came from inside -
—"Who is? Abbu!"
The old man replied in a trembling voice.

—"You stay inside, daughter. Don't come out here."

The old man made them stay in a room. His wife gave food and water to Ahmed and his companions. In the night they took out the wine, and started drinking.

A terrorist said-
—"I was thinking that there was a great lure in that girly voice."

The other said-
—"Then why not we use her...to calm our thrust. After all, our master has already told us what to do with the sisters and daughters of those bloody Indians."

There was lust in all of their eyes. Everyone knocked at the door of the inner room.

The old man asked-
—"what is the work?"

The terrorist said-
—"Listen, just come out, there's some work."

As soon as the door opened, all of them forcibly entered the inner room and stabbed the old man and his wife to death. They used cunningness, this time taking lessons from earlier, they did not fire the bullets.
The girl was about to scream but a terrorist closed her mouth by pressing with his hand. Then put a cloth in her mouth.

Suddenly the girl went numb to see her parents dying in front of her eyes. But Ahmed and his companions were not concerned about it. Those people tore the clothes of that girl. There was turn for everyone. Everyone took his turn to rape the poor girl. She couldn't even scream because of the cloth in her mouth. They kept on quenching their lust, the girl became exhausted. After that, the terrorists killed her too with knife. Thereafter, Ahmed and his companions went to another room and slept quietly.

It was foggy in the early morning. When he felt, Ahmed went for bathroom. A steel box was appeared placed in the corner. He expected that there would be some valuables in it. He took things out of it and started stacking them outside.

Some old coins, school identity card Ahmed.....Identity card Rukhsana.....Identity card of the old man and his wife......A group photo of the family....

Ahmed was sweating. So what... so what... was it his family? He killed his own parents! And with his own real sister.....he raped?
He felt dizzy and fainted. What had he done?
Then a voice was heard, the army had arrived there and a warning was made on the loudspeaker to surrender. But in Ahmed's hands, he no longer had the power to take up his rifle. He had committed many murders and loots, rapes, but today he was feeling bad for himself.

CHAPTER 6
THOSE CLOSENESS

Daksh was working in a private bank. He was not coming to office for many days. His mobile was also being switched off.

That day, it was late afternoon. The bank was very crowded. Even that day, Daksh had not reached the bank yet. His boss was very angry for his not coming to the office. He called another employee, Mr. Mehra.

The boss said angrily-

—"Mr. Mehra, Has Daksh not come to the office even today?"

Mr. Mehra replied-

—"No sir, and his mobile is also being switched off for many days."

The boss's anger turned to worry. He said-

—"Oh, this is very serious matter. Perhaps, His health may not be good. You take my driver, go to his flat and see."

Mr. Mehra nodded his head in agreement.

—"Ok sir, I'm going now."

Mr. Mehra reached Daksh's flat. The door of Daksh's flat was locked. He thought it appropriate to ask in the neighborhood-

—"Hey brother, this is Daksh's flat next door, isn't it?"

Neighbor replied-

—"Yes it is. You....?"

—"I'm from his office. He is not coming to the office these days. Here too the door is locked. Have you seen him?"

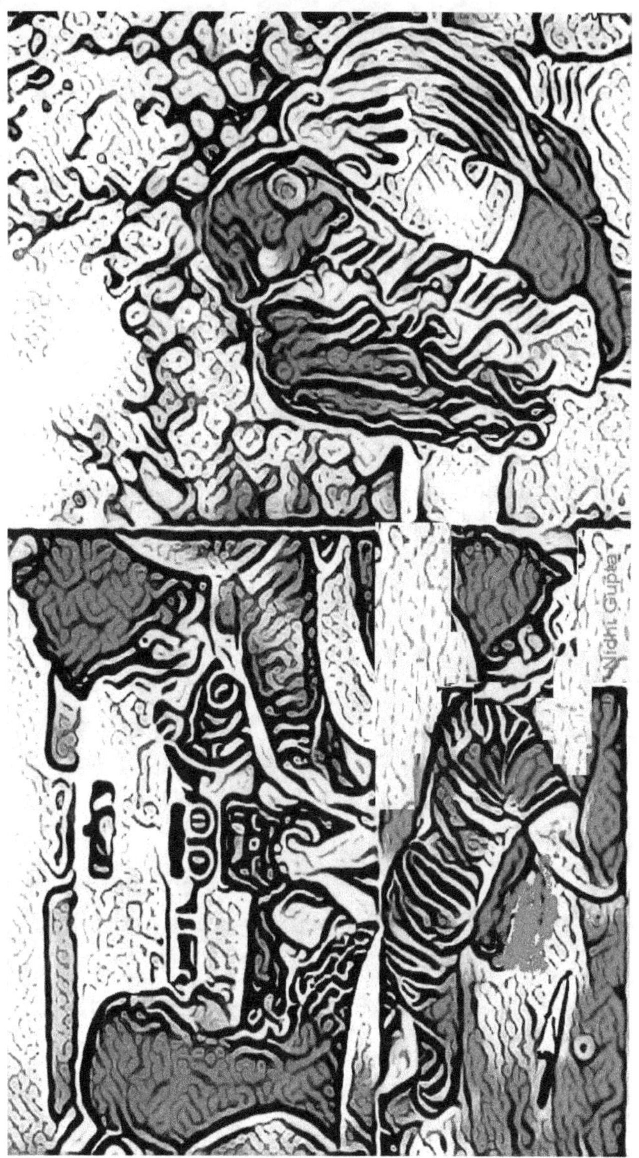

—"No, haven't seen him for a long time. He may have gone to his home in Indore."
Mr. Mehra also asked some other neighbors and guards, but nothing could be found.

Mr. Mehra got back. He told the boss. The people of the office first understood that he must have gone to his home in Indore.
Daksh was lived in that flat at Vishal Enclave society on rent. His family members were lived at Indore. While he was working in that private bank in Nagpur, His wife was working in the electricity department of Indore and lived in Indore. They could able to get meet only on holidays.
Later, the bankers contacted Daksh's family members over the phone. Mr. Mehra asked-
—"Hello, I am speaking from Daksh's office, from Nagpur. Am I talking to Daksh's father?"

From there Daksh's father had picked up the phone. He replied-
—"Yes, I am speaking father of Daksh myself. Tell me what's the matter."

—"Has Daksh come over there?"

Daksh's father was surprised at this question-
—"No, he will be there, I mean in Nagpur."

—"No… Daksh has not been coming to the office for the past several days. His mobile is also being switched off."

—"Isn't he even at his flat?"
Signs of worries appeared on forehead of Daksh's father.

—"No, his flat is locked, that's why I called you."

On coming to know that Daksh had not gone home, the bankers got filed a report in local police station thereby for missing of Daksh. The police enthusiastically started searching for Daksh. After much searching, his car was found parked on a deserted road. There was no one in the car. The policemen brought the car to the police station.

The policemen got his call details out. On the night of his disappearance, his last location was near Sainik Vihar Colony at night. Sainik Vihar Colony was a special colony for soldiers and their families. The police wondered what Daksh was doing around Sainik Vihar colony, and even at so late night.

The police went to Daksh's office for questioning. During interrogation, it was found that Daksh was a beau. He had an attractive personality. The stories of his affair with many girls in the office were famous. As soon as any new girl came, he would try to trap her. Sometimes he brought chocolates for them, sometimes some household items for them. Sometimes he taught them to drive vehicles. Girls also liked him because of his personality.

But the ill-effects of all these colorful mood swings of Daksh started falling on office work of Daksh. Sometimes he was busy in mobile, sometimes he was busy in talking and laughing with the girls of the office. His superiors had warned him many times about this.

During interrogation, the police found out that Varsha, a girl from the office, was lived in Sainik Vihar Colony. Her husband was serving in the army and his posting was on the border.
The police called Varsha for questioning. Asked her-

—"So, Miss Varsha, how long have you been working here?"

Varsha replied-
—"Excuse me, I am not Miss Varsha, I am Mrs. Varsha. And I've been here for almost a year."
There was hardness in the voice of Varsha.

The police again questioned-
—"How did you know Daksh?"

—"Daksh was my colleague. We used to work together, in the same office. Nothing more than that."

—"Daksh's last location was found near your house on the night of his disappearance. What is meant by that, what should be thought of it?"

— "I had learned driving car recently. And Daksh used to go in his car, afore of my car. So that I do not face any problem on the way. The same thing happened on that date of his disappearance."

The police recorded the statement and returned. But the police had still suspicion over Varsha. The Vishal Enclave where Daksha had his flat, was just behind Sainik Vihar colony. Police visited Sainik Vihar colony. There they checked the visitor register. Then their suspicion turned into belief.
Actually, too many times of Daksh's movement were recorded in the register, all for visiting to the house of Varsha. Many a days, both in the morning and in the evening.
The police arrested Varsha. The policemen started interrogation with Varsha. Inspector Vineet Ray and lady sub-inspector Noria were investigating the case.

Vineet Ray asked-
—"Yes, madam, Will now you tell graciously, why Daksh used to come to your place every day?"

Varsha said shouting-
—"I've told what I knew."

—"You told that Daksh used to go in his car, afore of your car. But getting the name registered in the visitor register of Sainik Vihar colony too may times, means that he used to visit your house regularly."

—"So what happened, we were both collogues. Whether colleagues' house is forbidden to visit?"

Vineet got angry-
—"It is not like that you are going to tell the truth so easily. Come here Noria."

Noria came there. Said-
—"Yes sir!"

Vineet said to Noria-
—"I am giving you time for the whole night. By the morning, she should be seen talking like a parrot."

Noria nodded her head as yes. Noria was skilled in getting women criminals to confess. She used all kinds of tricks. She did not let Varsha sleep the whole night.
—"Tell me, what was going on between you two? Where is Daksh?"

Varsha said making faces-
—"I don't know anything."

Noria pulled her up and gave her two hard slaps, and grabbing her hair, turned her whole head round. Varsha started crying. Tears welled up from her eyes. On rigorous interrogation, the Varsha broke, and this story came to the fore.

Daksh's brother was working in a government department in Nagpur itself. He had got a house from the government. Earlier, Daksh lived in the government house of his elder brother with family of elder brother. Then, after a rift with wife of his brother, he took a rented flat in the Vishal Enclave.

His parents were living in Indore. His wife was working in the electricity department of Indore and lived in Indore. Daksh lived alone in his flat and was depend on online food delivery companies and restaurants for food and drink.

On the other hand, Varsha lived in Sainik Vihar Colony. Her husband was serving in the army and his posting was on the border. She also lived alone in the house.

Earlier, Varsha used to come to the office by scooty. Then one day, she bought a car. Everyone in the office was congratulating her for new car. Daksh was also one of them-

—"Congratulations Varsha for the new car. When will you bring your car to the office?"

Varsha did not know how to drive. She told her problem to Daksh-

—"Thanks Daksh, I have bought the car, but I do not know how to drive."

—"It's okay, I'll teach you. I will come to your house every morning. In one week or ten days, you will learn for sure."

Then by the very next day, Daksh started teaching Varsha how to drive. He went to Varsha's house daily

for several days and taught her driving the car in Sainik Vihar colony itself.
—"Varsha, just press the clutch and put the gear, and then slowly release the clutch while pressing the accelerator."

Varsha did as Daksh said-
—"Wow, the car started moving."

Then, suddenly Daksh warned-
—"Varsha! Look to the front, you will hit the car with the pole."

Daksh grabbed the steering by the hand and moved it, on the same pretext, he touched Varsha's hand. Varsha didn't mind. Then Daksh got green signal. Sometimes he would hold Varsha's hand, sometimes on the pretext of telling the brakes, would put his hands on her thighs.
Within about fifteen days, Varsha perfectly learned driving car. But she was still afraid to bring the car to the office. Daksh encouraged her-
—"Now you have learned the car. Start coming to the office by car."

Varsha told-
—"There is a lot of traffic here. In a lot of crowds, I get nervous."

Daksh also found a solution for this and every day while coming to and going from office, Daksh used to go in his car, afore the car of Varsha, so that she would not face any problem on the way.
During this, both of them became good friends.
It was going on like that. Suddenly, the corona disease spread and a lockdown was imposed throughout the country. During the lockdown, Daksh had a big problem for food, as all the restaurants and food delivery

companies had stopped working. Whereas banks were open due to being an essential service.

One day it was afternoon. It was two o'clock, lunch time was going on. All the colleagues were busy in lunch. Daksh was eating Maggi instead of lunch. Varsha saw him eating Maggi. She asked-
—"What dude Daksh, you eat Maggi every day. Does your wife not give food?"

Daksh laughed and said-
—"Oh, that's not the point. Actually she is in Indore and working in electricity department. I don't know how to cook at all. Earlier, I thought that I will bring my wife from Indore. But the electricity department has been declared an essential service, and she has not got any leave."

Varsha said-
—"You know, I am solution for this problem. I will cook food for you. You don't need to eat Maggi by tomorrow."

By the next day onwards, Varsha started bringing tiffin for Daksh. Then a few days later, she started inviting Daksh to her house for breakfast and dinner as well. In the morning, Daksh would reach Varsha's house after getting ready from his house. Then, he would have breakfast there. Varsha would pack his tiffin along with her. Even in the evening, Daksh would eat food at her house.
But this relationship gradually turned into love. The reason was the loneliness of both. Daksha lived there away from his wife. His loneliness used to disturb him. He craved to talk to someone. Here Varsha's husband also did not come home for months. She would get bored living alone.

The closeness of both started growing. Every now and then Daksh reached Varsha's house and both would have quenched their lust.

As usual on the night of the incident, Daksh had come to Varsha's house after office and both were engrossed in making love. It was almost twelve in midnight. It was raining lightly outside. Then suddenly, the bell rang at the door. Varsha was surprised. Who came so late in night? She quickly put on her clothes, and then opened the door. There stood a man dressed in military clothes. He had an air bag in his hands. He said-
—"Surprise!!!"

—"Hey, you Dinesh?"
Varsha was shocked.

—"Yeah, me, oh let me in."
Dinesh said, taking off the bag from his shoulder. He was a little wet too due to rain outside."

Dinesh was the husband of Varsha. He had come home from the border suddenly, on leave. To surprise her, he had not even told Varsha about his coming.

Daksh, who was in another room, got alert on hearing the sound of the bell. He did not come out of that room.
Varsha gave Dinesh a towel. He went to the washroom of his bedroom to freshen up himself.
Until and immediately, Varsha hid Daksh in the store room of the house.
After that Varsha went to the kitchen. Varsha cooked the food. She served food to her husband.

Varsha said-
—"Hey, you surprised me, why should not you have made a call?"

Dinesh started laughing. Pointing finger at her, he said-
—" tell me, aren't you surprised, ha...ha...ha...."

Varsha said in surprise-
—"But how did you suddenly get the leave?"

Dinesh shrugged his shoulders and replied-
—"Just got it, somehow."

Dinesh was tired in the journey. After the meal, he went to sleep in the bedroom. Then as he fell asleep, Varsha went to the store room, to get Daksh out. She opened the door of the store room.

—"….Daksh…Daksh….Where is you?"
She whispered.

The room was in dark. She lit the light. But seeing the scene there, she cried out in fear.

Someone had killed Daksh with a knife. Daksh's dead body was lying in the room. A knife was lodged in his chest. Blood was oozing out and spread on the floor.

Her husband woke up after hearing the screams of Varsha. Running there searching for Varsha, he came to the store room. Varsha was stood there speechless. Sweat had gathered on her face.

—"What happened Varsha, what happened?"
Dinesh asked. He was surprised by her sudden scream.

—"…that….there..!"
Varsha stammered her finger, pointing to the corpse.

Dinesh asked in surprise-

—"Who is this man, and who killed him? Reply Varsha, why are you silent?"

Varsha replied-
—"I do not know. I had come here to get some stuff, in the time I saw, this dead body is lying here."
There was panic in the voice of the Varsha.

Dinesh was not a raw player, he had seen Daksh's pictures on WhatsApp, Facebook etc., in the group photos of the bank. He knew that Daksh was Varsha's colleague, however, he was not aware of his name.
Dinesh said in a stern voice-
—"Don't lie Varsha. I know he is your colleague. Will you tell me everything clearly, or I will call the police now."

On hearing the word "police", Varsha was horrified. spoke-
—"No... no. Don't call the police, I'll tell you everything."

Varsha, with due fear, confesses her husband about her and Daksh's illicit relationship. At first her husband got angry and beat her up. While beating her, he said-
—"You harlot, bastard, I was on the border taking my life on my hand, and you are doing whoredom here."

Varsha started pleading with folded hands-
—".....please... forgive me Dinesh, I have made a mistake. I don't know how I was deluded."

Dinesh's anger subsided only after beating her. When his anger cooled, he asked-
—"But why did you kill him?"

—"I didn't kill him, why would I kill him? I had come to get him out of here, so that he could go back to his home. But when I came here, I found him lying dead here."

Then something flashed in Varsha's mind that perhaps, Dinesh had seen Daksh and killed him. She asked-
—" Dinesh, perhaps you have done...... this murder....?"

Dinesh scolded her and said-
—"Shut up Varsha, I had gone to sleep in the room before your eyes. Then I didn't even come out."

Apologizing to the Dinesh, Varsha said-
—"Forgive me Dinesh, Please save me, I don't want to be accused of murder. I promise you that I will not make any such mistake in future."

Together they made a plan. They brought a meat cutting sharp knife from the kitchen. They Cut the corpse into several pieces with the help of that knife. Then after stuffing those pieces in sacks, they had put them in the trunk of their car. By then the rain had intensified. Both of them disposed the body in the forest behind Sainik Vihar Colony. Varsha and Dinesh did not use Daksh's car to dispose of the dead body. In doing so, they were in risk of being identified by others in the colony.
In the morning, Varsha carried Daksh's car by driving and left it on a deserted road.
The remains of the corpse, on the trails of the Varsha, were recovered from the forest behind Sainik Vihar Colony.

The police also arrested her husband. The police suspected that Dinesh might have come to know about Daksh and Varsha's relationship. And while Varsha was cooking food on the day of the incident, Dinesh lying on the pretext of sleepiness and exhaustion and sneaking into the store room covertly, would have stabbed Daksh

to death. Sub Inspector Noria started interrogating Dinesh-
—"Mr. Dinesh, your wife has told us everything. Remains of Daksh's body has also been recovered. Now, it will be in your best interest that you also confess."

Admitting his mistake, Dinesh said-
—"Inspector, my mistake was that I supported my wife in spite of her infidelity. Cut the corpse into several pieces and disposed it...."

Vineet Ray interrupted his saying and said-
—"And also murdered Daksh while he was hiding in the store room."

Dinesh said-
—"No, no, I didn't kill anyone. I was sleeping in my bedroom. Suddenly I heard the scream of Varsha, then I ran to the store room."

When neither Dinesh nor Varsha had confessed to the murder, even after a lot of questioning and third degree, the police decided to look at the matter with a fresh angle.

Inspector Vineet Ray was sitting on his seat thinking something, meanwhile Noria distracted him -
—"What are you thinking sir?"

Inspector Vineet Ray raised his head. Said to Noria-
—"I am thinking about any third person, who perhaps have killed Daksh. Both of them have not confessed killing Daksh as yet."

Noria asked-

—"Who could be the third person? There is a lot of security in Sainik Vihar Colony. How would anyone have reached there without entering visit in the register?"

Inspector Vineet Ray said-
—"Whatever it is, we have to start afresh, once again."

Police did search in Varsha's flat once again. But didn't find anything conclusive. Daksh's car, which Varsha had parked on a deserted road on the day of the incident, was searched again. Stepney and other tools were found missing from its trunk. Now the suspicion of the police was to any third person.
Inspector Vineet Ray went to the bank again and interrogated Daksh's co-workers. Took everyone's fingerprint samples and checked the CCTV.
It was found in the CCTV footage that, on that day Daksh had parked his car behind the bank building as the parking was full. In the afternoon, someone was found approaching to Daksh's car. In the footage of the evening, the same man was again seen walking towards Daksh's car. But in the evening, he was wearing different clothes. Daksha and Varsha went out together as usual, at 6 pm.
To confirm who that man was, the footage of the morning time on the day of the incident was taken out. Footage of everyone entering the office was seen.
A bank employee named Vikrant, was working in the same bank's office. Inspector Vineet Ray got suspicious on Vikrant. Because the color of the clothes of the person going towards Daksh's car, matched with the color of the clothes Vikrant wore that day. Moreover, the stature of both was also similar. However, the face of the person was unclear in the CCTV footage. Vikrant was present in the office that day, but he had left the office at 4 o'clock in the evening due to some personal work.

Fellow employees told that Vikrant was a very quiet person. But he was always worried and distressed. He was under the burden of work. Due to the workload, he used to get late every evening in getting out of the office for home.

Police arrested Vikrant on the basis of suspicion. The police started questioning him-

—"Mr. Vikrant, what were you doing that afternoon near Daksh's car?"

Vikrant replied-

—" I usually go for a little walk in the afternoon after lunch. That day, I might have gone to that side."

The police again asked him-

—"And, again in the evening, the reason for changing your clothes and going to the parking lot of the bank?"

Vikrant refused.

—"That's a wrong, I did not go to the bank's parking lot again."

—"Don't lie, we found your fingerprints inside the trunk of Daksh's car."

The police threw the dice, In fact the police did not find any fingerprints inside the trunk. But Vikrant got very upset after hearing this.

Seeing their trick being successful, the police interrogated him rigorously. During interrogation, Vikrant accepted the guilt of Daksh's murder. He told that he was jealous of Daksh.

Vikrant used to help women employees a lot, of which his fellow female employees would take a lot of advantage. They used to get their work done by him and straighten their owl. Due to all this, Vikrant's own work would have left undone, and he had to sit till late every day.

Not only this, the women employees of other branches of the bank, also kept asking him the solution of the problems on the phone. Being an experienced bank employee, he had solutions to many problems.

But all this was only to get their work done. Actually, no female employee could become his friend. Vikrant used to wonder how Daksh used to make women crazy after him. And here, even after doing all this for these female co-workers, it was to no avail.

After this, he came to know about the relationship between Varsha and Daksh. Out of jealousy, he decides to kill Daksh.

On the day of the murder, Vikrant secretly overhears Varsha and Daksh's conversation. He came to know that Daksh was to go to Varsha's house that day again. He reached Daksh's table at noon. It was a lunch time. Daksh was not on his chair at that time. On Daksh's table, the key of Daksh's car was lying. Vikrant secretly picked up the keys of Daksh's car. He went to Daksh's car and opened the trunk of the car. Since it was lunchtime, all the staff members went out to the canteen to take lunch and sip tea, so no one got suspicious.

From the trunk, he took out the stepney, cover, and tools, and put those in his own car, so that there could be enough place to sit in the trunk of Daksh's Car. Then he put a piece of adhesive tape on the lock of the trunk and dropped the door of the trunk. Due to this, the door of the trunk was shut down, but because the tape was being attached, it could not be locked. After this he took the key of the car back and placed it on Daksh's table.

In the evening, Vikrant left the office at 4 o'clock on the pretext of urgent work. He parked his car on the side of the road leading to Sainik Vihar. He had changed clothes in his car so that no one could recognize him.

Then he came back with an taxi. Then he secretly sat in the trunk of Daksh's car.

Since Daksh used to come office by four wheeler singularly, he would rarely open the trunk. In case of buying the some articles, he would have kept it in the backseat of his car. In such a situation, the chances of opening the trunk were very low.

That day, Daksh and Varsha left the office at 6 pm. Daksh put his bag on the back seat and started the car. The car started going towards Sainik Vihar. Varsha was in her car behind the car of Daksh. The two reached the house of Varsha at Sainik Vihar colony.

When both went inside the house, Vikrant came out of the trunk. He had taken a bag with him. In which, there were a knife, screwdriver, chloroform spray, etc., so that it could come in handy in case of need. He started looking for a way to enter inside the house. The sky was cloudy that day and it was very mugginess in environment. Because of the humidity, the Varsha had opened a window of the house. The window grills were attached with the help of screws. When it got dark, Vikrant opened the grill with the help of the screwdriver and entered in the house. Then, he went into the store room and hid.

Then, upon the arrival of her husband, the Varsha made Daksh hidden in the store room. However, Vikrant was hiding behind an old fridge lying in the store room, due to which Daksh could not see him.

Varsha was with her husband at that time. Vikrant sneaked out from behind the fridge. He had carried a spray of chloroform, so that Daksh could not make a noise. He first sprayed the anesthetic, due to which Daksh became unconscious. After this, Vikrant killed Daksh by stabbing him with the knife. Then, Vikrant went back and got out through the window. He fitted the grill back with the help of the screwdriver. After this, he went and hid in the trunk of Daksh's car again. Later, the next morning, Varsha drove the car and left it on a deserted road. From there Vikrant went back to his house.

The police registered the case and sent Vikrant to the jail. Varsha and her husband were booked for tampering with evidences and destroying the dead body.

CHAPTER 7
REVENGE OF LOVE

It was seven' o clock in the morning. Inspector Vijay was sipping tea, sitting on his chair at the police station. On the table in front of him, several files were lying. A short distance away was the Constable's chair, on which the Constable was drowsing seated there.

At the time, a car stopped outside the police station. A woman got out of the car. She, almost running, went straight to Inspector Vijay.

She said in a nervous voice-

—"Inspector, I have to get filed missing report of my husband."

The inspector put down the glass of tea. He looked at the woman. The woman was looking terrified. She was wearing an expensive saree. And jewelry too. But the hair was in disarray, as if she was in a hurry. The matter seemed serious. Inspector asked-

—"Your name....?"

—"Nirmala."

—"Address?"

—"421 Vijay Colony."

—"Tell me in detail how long since your husband has been missing?"

—"My husband has a business of paint and building material. His name is Ravikant. He didn't come back from the shop last night. His mobile is not working either. Earlier, it was telling out of reach, then the switch off message started coming."

Saying this, the woman started crying.

Nidhi Gupta

Inspector Vijay consoles her-
—"Don't be upset. It is possible that he must have stayed with some friend anywhere. The mobile battery may have run out."

But Nirmala was very worried. She said-
—"Earlier, I also thought that he must have gone somewhere with any of his friends. But I inquired with all the acquaintances, He were nowhere to be found."

The woman started crying out loud again.
Vijay asked for water and made her drink. Then told her-
—"Don't panic. We will go looking for your husband. Tell me if he has any enmity with anyone, or you have any doubts on someone?"

—"No, there was no such thing."

—"Has there been a threatening phone call or a demand for money?"

—"Nope."

—"Give any latest photo of your husband and get his appearance noted to the constable."

The woman had brought her husband's photo. She gave the photo to the Constable and went away after get him written her husband's description.

Inspector Vijay first went to the market where Ravikant's shop was. Ravikant's shop was in a crowded market place. Inspector Vijay interrogated nearby. There was a weekly closure last day. But Ravikant, as usual, kept the shop open from 4 pm onwards because in the business of building materials, the customers kept needing something or the other.

Then, Inspector Vijay went to Ravikant's shop. In that busy market, it was a big shop. Ravikant had taken a paint agency, which was going very well. Apart from this, he also kept a lot of building materials and sanitary items.
The shop was open. Even in the absence of the owner, the servants opened the shop by bringing another key from the house. There were 5 servants in the shop. Inspector Vijay started questioning with them-
—"Which time did this shop close yesterday?"

A servant told-
—"Last night the shop closed at around 7 pm. We all went out together."

Inspector again asked-
"How did your boss go?"

The servant replied-
—"He sent his driver back with his car, and went walking on foot."

Ravikant used to come by car. But in the evening, as the shop was not far away, he would often walk home on foot. That day too, he had sent the driver back, and went walking on foot.

Inspector Vijay searched the shop. Checked in the CC TV as well. But it only had scenes of the shop closing and exiting. He didn't get any clues.

Nirmala had told that, last time she had a talk with her husband, on the date of missing, at 6.30 pm. Vijay got the call details and location of Ravikant from the mobile company. The last call was shown at 6.30 pm on

Nirmala's number. While the last location was shown at Manakpur, at the time of 10 o'clock in the night.

Now, the question was arising that what Ravikant was doing in Manakpur, at ten o'clock in the night? Since he had sent the driver back with the car, it was clear that either he had gone there with someone else, or someone forcibly took him to Manakpur.

Manakpur was a village 80 km away from the city. Inspector Vijay suspected kidnapping. But till the time, no call had come for the ransom. Nor any threat call was received before his disappearance.

Inspector Vijay inquired at Manakpur police station, and narrating everything, sent Ravikant's photo and appearance by e-mail.

Two days later, a call came on wireless from Manakpur police station. A dead body was found there. Inspector Vijay immediately left for Manakpur. But that body turned out to be that of a local citizen. Perhaps, he was hit by a speeding vehicle on the highway. The date of the accident in the postmortem report was - October 11, the day Ravikant went missing. Inspector Vijay returned. There was an atmosphere of anger among the local businessmen due to the kidnapping of Ravikant. They met the commissioner and threatened to agitate in front of the police station. The commissioner summoned Inspector Vijay.

The commissioner asked for the status of the case-
—"What happened to this Ravikant kidnapping case?"

Inspector Vijay replied-
—"The investigation is going on. But there is no clue to be found."

The commissioner advised to him-
—"Look Vijay, I want results, that too soon. The local traders are very angry because of this case."

Inspector Vijay said-
—"I will try to solve it as soon as possible, sir."

The commissioner asked Vijay to solve the case within a week.

Inspector Vijay again thought of searching Ravikant's shop. This time he checked again the CCTV installed there. In it, Ravikant was seen leaving the shop, but nothing more was known.
Inspector Vijay was disappointed. He didn't understand, where to look for clues? He happened to walk from there, suddenly his eyes fell on another shop on the same road.
That shop also had installed a CC TV camera. Inspector Vijay reached there. He asked the owner of that shop to show the CCTV footage of October 11-
—"How long have you had this CC TV here?"

The shopkeeper replied-
—"Long ago, sir, what's the matter?"

Inspector Vijay said-
—"I am investigating the disappearance of Ravikant, a paint businessman here. I want to see the footage of October 11, of the camera outside here."

The shopkeeper said-
—"Yeah, take a look. On that day, our shop was closed due to weekly closure. But this camera is always on. Ravikant is a fine man, whatever possible to me, I will cooperate."

Then, looking at the servant, the shopkeeper shouted-
—"O Ramu, go and bring tea for Inspector sir."

Inspector Vijay started looking carefully at the footage of the CC TV.

This time his effort was successful. 3 people were making Ravikant sit in a white Maruti van on the point of the gun. But due to the distance, the face of persons and the number of the Maruti van were unclear. But it was clear from this that, Ravikant had been kidnapped.

Since the last location of the mobile was at Manakpur, it was quite possible that the kidnappers had crossed the toll plaza on the way with Ravikant. There was no other way to reach Manakpur. Inspector Vijay got the details out of the Rohini toll plaza falling before Manakpur.

On the night of the kidnapping, at that time, 17 Maruti vans had passed by.

Out of this, 12 were of white colour. Inspector Vijay got the names of the owners of all those vehicles from road transport agency.

One of them had recently sold the van to someone named Amarjeet. The buyer had not yet got registered the vehicle in his name. Generally, in kidnapping etc., either a stolen vehicle is used or a vehicle purchased second hand. Criminals do not get done registration and name transfer after purchase of vehicle. Then, after using the vehicle in a crime, the vehicle is either destroyed or left abondoned.

Inspector Vijay reached to the house of the former owner of the Van. The former owner of the car was questioned-

—"Did you have car of this number?"

The owner of the car was confused. He said-
—"Yes, but what happened?"

Inspector Vijay told-
—"This vehicle has been used for criminal purposes."

The former owner of the car was shocked-

—"Oh my god, but I had sold the car a long time ago."

—"How did you sell, any paper?"

—"Yes, sold through a paper agreement here, which is called Chirkut in the local language. There is such trend here. The buyer, whose name was Amarjeet, had said that he would get the registration done in his name. Here's the paper..."

The former owner of the car took out the paper and showed it. Vijay checked the paper. He felt it appropriate and according to the rules.

That buyer was unknown to the former owner. The name of the new buyer of the vehicle was being told as Amarjeet. Amarjeet's mobile number was found with the former owner of the vehicle. On searching, it was found that it was in the name of another person Arun. The number was now switched off.

However, call records has been got taken out from the mobile company. And from that, the information of many calls were received.

The main people in communication with the mobile number were persuaded, and were brought to the police station for questioning. On everyone's trail, a man named Sikandar was arrested.

After this, a story came out, which was related to the previous life of Ravikant's wife, Nirmala. About ten years ago, when Ravikant's wife Nirmala was studying in a famous college in her city.

One day, she was studying with other students in the class. It was an important lecture.

Then suddenly came the sound of shouting slogans. Student union election was near. A leader came inside wearing a kurta pajama jacket. He was wearing a garland of flowers.

Back and forth, his comrades also entered the class shouting slogans. He pushed the professor to the side. Now the leader introduced himself. It was student leader Amjad Khan. He appealed to everyone to vote for his side-
—"Brothers and sisters, this year I am contesting the student union election for the post of president. I apologize for interrupting your studies. I am a leader attached to the ground, whatever problem you have, feel free to tell me. I will go to any extent to help you."
Then the disciples standing behind clapped, and Amjad and his companions went out shouting slogans.

During her college days, Nirmala was known as a beautiful girl. Every boy was eager to befriend her. Among them was student leader Amjad Khan.

Because of Nirmala's beauty, a boy Gaurav started teasing Nirmala again and again. Nirmala started getting very upset. One day she came to college wearing in jeans clothes, and was looking very gorgeous. The boy blocked her way in the campus, and singing loudly, said-
—"Wow, hi, you are causing havoc in these beautiful jeans clothes."

Nirmala said angrily-
—"Shut up rude, you guys come here to study or to look at girls' clothes."

The boy said rudely-
—"Oh, This anger, on this I want to die. You must have come for study here in college, I only come to see you."

A college girl advised her to meet Amjad Khan. Amjad Khan used to give small help to the students to make impression among students. Nirmala met Amjad. told-
—"Amjad, I need your help."

Amjad asked-
—"Say, How can I help you?"

—"That…Gaurav bothers me on and off."
Nirmala coyly told him the whole thing.

Amjad assured her-
— "It doesn't matter, he won't bother you from today onwards, rest assured. I will explain it to him in my own language."

Amjad thrashed the boy who was molesting Nirmala and warned him-
—"After today, if you ever be seen near Nirmala, then I will break your legs."

—"I'm sorry, I won't go after her anymore."
Gaurav started pleading with folded hands.

After this incident, Amjad Khan became a hero for Nirmala. Amjad Khan was already hooked on her.
Amjad had arranged a small party in the college on Valentine's Day. The dance program was going on. Nirmala was sitting quietly on the side eating something. Amjad Khan came towards her and invited her for dance-
—"Hello Nirmala, can we dance together?"
—"Why not."
Nirmala said smiling and happily agreed.

Both came on the dance floor. Now, there was slow ball dance music playing. Amjad placed his hand on Nirmala's waist. Nirmala placed her hand on Amjad's shoulder. Both started dancing.

On that day, Nirmala was wearing an attractive pink colored gown. In which, her beauty was getting more and more exhibited. Seeing the opportunity, Amjad said-
—"You're very beautiful."

Nirmala was stunned. No one had talked to her like that earlier. Her cheeks turned red. She didn't know how to answer. Then she said-
—"Thank you."

Both danced very fabulously. After the dance, both of them came together to have dinner. There was a buffet system in the party, but Amjad got arranged a separate table set up for her. He engaged four waiters to serve. During the meal, there was a lot of conversation between the two. Amjad asked-
—"What do you like to eat?"

Nirmala picked up the chicken piece and said-
—"Tandoori Chicken."

—"I thought you were a veg."
Amjad looked at her in surprise.

—"Everyone in my house is pure vegetarian. But I eat non-veg while outside."
Nirmala spoke while chewing the words with chicken pieces.

Amjad a bit being un-formal, said-
—"You're so beautiful, do you have any boyfriend?"

Nirmala looked at him in surprise. Then said-
—"No. I am a bit conservative. First studies, then career, then all these things."

Amjad proposed-

—"Can we be friends? I like you very much."

—"Why not?"
Nirmala gladly accepted the friendship.

Then, they started meeting every day. There was a park near the college. The specialty of the park was that boys and girls would come to meet there, and would get the experience of being romeo-juliet under the trees. Amjad and Nirmala also started meeting there.
Then the closeness started to increase even more. Both started meeting secretly by bunking the classes.
In the election of the student union, Amjad had entrusted her with the command of campaigning among women. Nirmala campaigned loudly for Amjad. She cited the example of beating a boy, who was teasing her. Nirmala gathered female students and held meetings. She said while delivering a speech-
—"We girls come here to study, while we have to face molestation and other things here. We should choose a leader who can help us, protect us. Amjad Khan not only helps us when we need it all the time, but he is also capable of answering the hooliganism. I appeal to you that all of you, make him victorious by giving your valuable vote."

Amjad became very popular among women, because of Nirmala. As a result, Amjad won the election.
On the day of the election victory, Amjad gave a grand party. There was going a lot of music and fooding till late night. Nirmala had come to the party on the excuse of "I will study in the night with my friend" at her house.
After everyone left, only Nirmala and Amjad were remained in the party. Amjad proposed Nirmala that night.
He had brought a gold ring. He put the ring in finger of Nirmala and asked-

—"I love you very much. Will you be my love? I will fulfill your every wish. I'll keep you happy for whole of my life."

Nirmala liked Amjad from the very beginning. She immediately agreed-
—"I also like you Amjad, but I could never tell you. I was afraid that you might refuse."

Both kissed each other. That day, along with Amjad, Nirmala had also drank a little. In such a condition, it did not feel right for her to go home. Therefore, at Amjad's suggestion, she accompanied Amjad to his friend's farmhouse. Both reached the farmhouse, but suddenly the weather got bad there, it started raining along with the storm. After getting down from the car to reaching the room at farmhouse, both of them got drenched. In the meantime the power to the farm house went out. Both took out their clothes and put them to dry. The confession and agreement had already taken place. Some inebriation was in alcohol, some was in foul weather. After this, both of them also had a physical relationship there. In the morning, Amjad dropped Nirmala to her house.

But now it has started. Often the two would meet in hotels and quench the body's lust. Because of Amjad's influence, he would get rooms without Identity Card. Amjad used to get Nirmala's attendance done in college too.
But all this started affecting Nirmala's studies. One, her absence in class almost daily, secondly, instead of studying, Amjad used to roam around in her mind. As a result, she failed in the next exam.
Nirmala's family members were quite surprised. Because Nirmala was very good in studies. Some doubts had been arisen in their minds about Nirmala. They started keeping an eye on her. When the details

were extracted from her mobile, they come to know that Nirmala has a lot of conversations with Amjad.

Nirmala's friend was Zahra. Zahra was a very intelligent girl. She was confidante of Nirmala. Nirmala used to tell everything about her to Zahra. Zahra had already forbade Nirmala to have a physical relationship with Amjad. Nirmala's father asked taking her in confidence, and then Zahra told the whole thing.

Nirmala's father was stunned. He beat up Nirmala. Scolded her and said-
—"We send you to study in college, and you go there for blowing tulips."

Nirmala said with folded hands-
—"Dad, forgive me. I was turned on wrong way. But Amjad is a very nice boy. We both love each other..."

The father cut her point, then scolded-
—"You shameless, keep quiet! You are not ashamed to talk like this in front of the your father. I am stopping your college going from today. You will not even step out from home. Beware, if your even tried to meet Amjad again... It will not be good."

Then Nirmala was banned to go out from house. Nirmala and Amjad, both started yearning to meet each other. First Amjad Khan's unemployment, secondly his involvement in politics and hooliganism, Nirmala's family members did not like him. They were strongly against this relationship.

One day Amjad came to Nirmala's house, and in front of Nirmala's father, he proposed for marriage with Nirmala. Amjad said-

—"Babuji, me and your daughter, love each other very much. And we want to get married."

Nirmala's father flatly refused-
– "Look Amjad, you cannot marry Nirmala. She is studying at the time. It is my advice also to you that you should leave the affair of love and focus on your career."

Amjad said-
—"I am a student leader now. If I contest elections, I can win and become MLA or MP in future. I promise that I will keep your daughter happy by all means."

Nirmala's father replied-
—"Whatever it is, we are traditional people. My daughter's marriage will take place where I will decide."

Amjad got furious at Nirmala's father's refusal. He threatened Nirmala's father to do something wrong with him. After Amjad's departure, Nirmala's father became very worried.
One day Amjad was staging a sit-in agitation with the students outside the office of the Vice-Chancellor of the university. During the sloganeering, he started entering the office, raising provocative slogans against the Vice-Chancellor. When the guard tried to stop, Amjad manhandled him. Amjad and his companions start sabotaging there. The Vice-Chancellor called the police.
The police arrested Amjad and sent him to jail. The police produced CCTV footage as evidence in the court, on the basis of which the court sentenced Amjad for six months imprisonment.
Nirmala's father felt that this was a good opportunity, and he persuaded Nirmala to get marry with Ravikant, a businessman who had a good business, house and car.
Amjad did not even know about the marriage at the time. When he came out after six months of imprisonment, he

again got engrossed in the politics. Many girls came and went in his life, but he could not forget Nirmala.
Then, one day Amjad came to know about Nirmala. Nirmala had come to a shopping mall to do some shopping. Amjad also went there to buy something. Nirmala was busy in buying something, that's when someone put a hand on her shoulder from behind-
"How are you Nirmala?"

Nirmala turned back. Seeing Amjad, she got speechless. Now, there was maturity on Amjad's face. He had grown a beard. But as before, he was in kurta pajama and jacket.
Nirmala did not understand what she should say. Then, she collected herself. Said-
—".....Hey you Amjad,... I'm fine."

The two went to a nearby coffee shop to chat. Both sat silent for a long time. Amjad picked up the menu card and extended it towards Nirmala. Asked-
—"What will you take Nirmala?"

She remained silent.

He asked again-
—"Coffee?"

Nirmala shook her head and said yes with a gesture. She was finding it very difficult to stay calm. She got up from her chair and said-
—"I just come through the washroom."

In the washroom, she closed the door from inside, and started weeping bitterly. Then, she controlled herself. Her mascara was overflowing with tears. She washed her face with water. Then, taking out the makeup kit from her purse, she cleaned up her face. After that, she came back at table and sat down on the chair.

Waiter put Nirmala's favorite latte coffee and garlic bread on the table and left. She looked up at Amjad. Amjad still remembered his choice.
Then, they had a normal conversation. Nirmala told him about her marriage while Amjad was in the jail.

Amjad complained-
—"You didn't wait for me even for some time."

Nirmala told her helplessness. Then said-
—"You know, Amjad, sometimes circumstances are not in your hands. Then one has to accept the circumstances."

Nirmala kept crying a lot even after coming home. That day, her husband had gone out of town somewhere. She started remembering her old days, Spent with Amjad,. Sometimes she would get angry at her father, sometimes at herself. She also began to regret for her marriage. Then, her eyes fell on Ravikant's photograph hanged on the wall. She started remembering some of her father's lessons. Ravikant did not let her down any time. She had received a lot of love, jewellery, money, car and all those things which a woman craves from her husband. Her father, perhaps, had done everything right in his own opinion.

Amjad met her again after a few days and talked about starting the relationship again-
—"Can we make a fresh start again? Can you leave everything and come to me again?"

Nirmala refused-

—"No, Amjad, you were my first love. I really loved you. But now I belong to someone else. It is also a sin for me to think of anyone else other than my husband."

Amjad said in a very beseeching voice-
—"Have you ever thought, that how would I live without you?"

Nirmala also became emotional and started weeping. Then, wiping away her tears, she said-
—"Yes, I have thought, you forget me and settle your household with someone else."

Amjad Khan had already started politics, but he was still a follower of leaders instead, and could not achieve any position. His work was going on only on the strength of hooliganism. In such a situation, Nirmala refused to leave her husband, who had no shortage of comforts, and denied to go with Amajd.
This refusal made Amjad furious. There was a person named Sikandar in his gang. Amjad gave him money, with which Sikandar bought a second hand Maruti van.
Taking the same Maruti van along, Sikandar, Amjad and their companions first tracked down Ravikant. When he comes, when he goes, which way he passes, all have been known to them.
Then on the day of the incident, when Ravikant got his shop closed and left for home on foot. Amjad, along with his three other accomplices, followed him. First due to weekly Closure, the second due to time to close the shop, so there was silence and emptyness. At one point, Amjad obstructed Ravikant. Amjad threatened Ravikant with gun-
—"come with us quietly. Even if you try to make noise or manipulate, you will be killed."

Ravikant had no choice but to obey him. He was kidnapped.

But, there Amjad made a mistake. In a hurry, he could not turn off Ravikant's mobile.

Earlier their plan was to demand a ransom for him and thereafter they would kill him. For this, they took him to Manakpur. While driving very fast on the Highway to Manakpur, they blew up a man.

Suddenly, Amjad noticed Ravikant's mobile just before Manakpur border. And those people broke his mobile and burnt it.

When the information reached to the police at Manakpur police station, Amjad took Ravikant out of there.

On the way in the forest, there was a natural pond. Amjad killed Ravikant there with a knife and cut the body into pieces and put it in the same pond. In the pond, he put piranha, foreign mangur and other carnivorous fish.

The police arrested Amjad Khan. On his trail, the pond situated in the forest was searched. Fragments of human bones and a skull were found in it. The meat was all eaten by the fish.

The knife thrown in the pond also found by the police, with which Amjad had killed Ravikant.

Nirmala got a lifetime widowness as a gift of love at a young age.

Ravikant, who had no fault in all this, got death.

Amjad Khan and his 3 accomplices were sent to jail after being tried for kidnapping, murder and criminal conspiracy.

CHAPTER 8
MURDER OF THE FATHER

On the evening of July 7, 47-year-old Ehsan called his 3 daughters Fatima, Mariam and Qutubunissa to his room. He was very angry, whilst the girls were very scared.
Ehsan had an old house. It was small. He had put a cot in the verandah. There were two rooms, in one Ehsaan used to sleep, in the other his daughters. Naima was Ehsan's wife, who had died a long time ago.
Ehsan scolds the threes for not cleaning the verandah properly-
—"I want to know why the verandah was not cleaned there?"

Mariam said-
—"It was broomed in the morning, and wiped also."

Ehsan's voice intensified-
—"Then how are these leaves and dust lying here? I have told all of you many times that I do not tolerate filth."

Fatima said-
—"The wind is blowing since morning and it is autumn. It is natural for leaves and dust to come in."

Ehsaan, hearing her reasoning, got furious with anger. He started shouting-
—"You are doing arguments to your father? Wait, let me teach you a lesson now."

And then Ehsaan searched for something nearby, there was a chili-sprinkler in front. He opened its lid completely. Then, he throw chili powder on the faces of the three girls. A considerable part of the chili went into

the eyes of the three girls. The girls began to torment with intense burning and pain.

The girls, screaming, immediately ran towards the courtyard. There they kept washing their eyes for a long time with the water in the tub. Then the burning in the eyes subsided.

On that night, soon after, when Ehsan was asleep, the girls attacked on him with knives, hammers and other household items, inflicting fatal wounds on Ehsan's head, neck and chest.

In the morning when he died, the three girls reached to the police station.

Duty was changed in the police station early in the morning. The constable was sitting in the police station drinking tea. Seeing the girls helter-skelter at police station, he asked-

—"Hey, what happened?"

Qutubunissa replied-
—"There has been a murder in our house."

—"...Murder?...whose?"

—"Our father's."

—"Who killed?"

In response, Qutbunissa started looking at Fatima. Fatima said firmly-
—"All three of us, we have come here to surrender."

The Constable immediately took them to the Inspector. Hearing the whole thing, the inspector went out towards house of those girls. There lay the corpse of a 47-year-old man with various wounds on his body. The inspector got panchnama (Paperwork) done of the body and sent the body for the postmortem. The whole house was sealed. The three girls were taken into police custody.

Inquiries and investigations soon uncovered a history of extensive violence in the family. Ehsan repeatedly beat, tortured, kept them inmates and sexually abused all three of his daughters for many years.

Earlier, it used to be a happy family. Ehsan and his wife Naima. It was a small house. This house was the ancestral home of Ehsan, which came to his share after his father's death. Ehsan used to run a small shop in a nearby market. Sufficient money came from the shop for food and clothes.

Naima gradually became the mother of two daughters. Ehsan was not happy when the second daughter was born. He said-

—"What is this? A daughter again born to us. We have so much poverty, and over and above this burden has also come."

There was despair in his voice.

—"Why do you say that? Why will our daughter be a burden on us? We will get her educated, make her study, make her stand on her feet."

Naima tried to convince him.

But Ehsan was not ready to listen to anything. He said-

—"But whatever you say, whatever you do, she will go to her husband's house finally! Or will you keep them on your chest for the whole of your life? Had the son been there, he would have been the support of old age"

Ehsan still hoped that the third child would be a son. While Naima did not want to have a third child, the reason was her deteriorating health and the financial condition of the household. But in front of Ehsan's insistence, she was compelled.

When the third child also born as daughter, Ehsan's patience broke. He started drinking heavily. At home, he used to beat Naima and curse her for the birth of daughters.

Due to his drinking habit, there had been a severe shortage of money in the house.

Ehsan started cursing Naima-

—"You have ruined my dreams. I was dreaming of a son, you again gave birth a daughter, to put burden on my chest. We have so much poverty, if we have son, he would support me in business, if not today, perhaps after ten years. Get feed, teach these girls and then spend big money in dowry."

Naima tried to explain her best-

—"Ehsaan, what are you saying, these daughters are also your own blood. And you, who spend all this money on alcohol? If you stop drinking alcohol, then we may eat and live with dignity."

But Ehsan started shouting at Naima-

—"I drink with my own earnings, not your father's...."

Naima was very weak while giving birth to the third child. At first, the doctor had advised her to have an abortion, as her life could be in danger during the delivery, but Ehsan did not allow it to happen. Naima had to be operated for delivery. The lives of both the mother-child were saved, but Naima became unable to be mother again. Ehsan used to blame Naima for this also.

Naima used to convince to Ehsaan that he should give up his alcohol addiction and concentrate on his business. Take good care of his daughters. Where nowadays even son and daughter-in-law do something for the parents? But all this had no effect on Ehsan.

One day, like this, there was a fight in the night and in the morning Naima committed suicide. Her body was found hanging with the fan.
Mariam went for Bathroom. And the other two girls were sleeping. Mariam was the first who saw Naima hanging with the fan.
She started crying-
—" Father, Father, look what happened to the mother?"

Mariam made a noise, calling first the father and sisters, then the neighbors. There was crying and crying.
With the help of neighbours, the body was pulled down from the fan. There was a crowd gathered there. Somebody informed the police.
Police came. The body was sent for post-mortem.
The daughters told the police that their mother could not have committed suicide. Fatima spoke to the police inspector-
—"There was a disagreement in the house, but my mother was not one of those who committs suicide, sir."

The inspector asked-
—"Do you suspect someone?"

What does Fatima tell? She gave a short answer-
—"Nope."

The police searched the whole house. No suicide note was found. By the way, Naima was not so educated enough. Neighbors told about Ehsan and Naeema's quarrel. The police took Ehsan for interrogation, kept him in lockup for almost a week. They asked a lot with him-
—"Speak, why did you kill your wife?"

Ehsan started crying-
—"Why would I kill, sir? I loved her so much."

The inspector said-
—"We have come to know that you used to beat her."

Ehsan replied-
—"It was sometimes, when I drink sir, we used to fight…."

The inspector interrupted his saying in the middle and said-
—"And you killed her after the fight that day."

Ehsan started crying again-
—"No no, Mommy swear, I didn't kill her. Leave me sir, I have three little daughters, I don't know how they are. Have they eaten anything or not…."

With no evidence, any case could not be made out against him. Ehsan was released for the sake of the little girls. The file was closed considering the case as a suicide.

After the death of his wife, Ehsan wanted to remarry, but none of the men agreed to give his daughter to an alcoholic and disgraced man. He talked to an old man in the locality who was an expert in arranging marriages. It has been a long time of talking, but nothing has happened. Ehsaan's patience became exhausted, so he went to find the old man. It was 2'O clock in the afternoon. At that time, the old man was resting on a handcart in the market. Ehsaan wakes him up hesitantly. Asked him-
—"Baba, Baba, did you talk anywhere?"

The old man said rubbing his eyes-
—"I have made a talk with some, but they were not ready because of your drinking habit."

Ehsan tried to explain-
—"I have given up alcohol. Sometimes, I take it to forget the tension. After marriage, I will leave it completely."

The old man asked-
—"You have three daughters. Who will take the responsibility of handling them?"

Ehsan insisted-
—"Hey, all the three of them do all the household chores themselves. I am telling you, any woman who comes here, will certainly enjoy the queenship."

—"Okay, I will see."
The old Baba said with a view to get rid of.

—"Widow and even a divorcee will be accepted, Baba."

But Ehsan's dream of second marriage could not be fulfilled. For this also, he also believed his dead wife and his three daughters guilty.
After Naima's death, tyranny of Ehsan had been increased. He would beat up the three daughters by calling them in a different room on some pretext or the other. He threatened to kill them. At that time, the age of the three daughters Fatima Mariam and Qutubunnisha were nine, seven and five years respectively. All three were very scared and could not resist anything.

Slowly the days passed and the eldest daughter Fatima turned seventeen and she reached the threshold of youth. Now, Ehsan used to stare at her with strange eyes. He told Fatima one day-
—"You will take the place of your mother, I will marry you and you will give birth a son to me."

At first Fatima thought that Ehsaan was grumbling anything in drunk, but later she realized that she was wrong. One day when Fatima was dressing up in the room after taking a bath, Ehsaan forcibly entered the room and started touching her inappropriately.

On this Fatima got very scared. She pushed Ehsaan hard and shouted-
—"What are you doing father? Move out."

And Fatima went to another room. But since then, Fatima was very scared. Whenever she saw Ehsaan, she would walk away from him. She could feel his eyes staring at her body.

After this one day, Ehsaan sent both the younger daughters out to get grocery. Fatima was alone in the house. She was hand-sewing some clothes in her room. Suddenly, Ehsaan secretly went to her room. Fatima was shocked to see him. She asked-
—"Need something, papa?"

—"….no….yes…., waa… water… give water."
Ehsaan almost stammered.

Fatima brought water. On the moment, Ehsan was standing near the door. He closed the door as soon as Fatima entered in room.
Fatima was terrified. She shouted and said-
—"What are you doing, Father? Why did you close the door?"

Lust was visible in Ehsan's eyes, he said-
—"You'll find out now."

Ehsan caught Fatima. Fatima kept crying. Ehsan tore her clothes.

Fatima said crying-
—"I am your daughter. You are my father, how can you do this to me."

But in the blindness of lust, Ehsaan had forgotten everything pertaining to the relationship. He raped her. Then, leaving her crying, he went out. When Mariam and Qutubunissa came from the market, they found Fatima sobbing in torn rags. She was in great shock and sat on the ground, looking at the void. Both the sisters asked together-
—"What happened to you? Your such condition....."

In response, Fatima could not say anything. Mariam went running and brought water. Fatima was made drink the water with great difficulty. She with weeping, told her sisters about the action of her father.
All three girls started crying.
—"If mother was alive, all this would not have happened to us."

Then looking at the sky, the three girls wept and said-
—"Mommy, why did you leave us and went away. You would have taken us with you too."

Then it became a daily routine for Ehsaan. Earlier, he used to beat them up, now he started sexually abusing all the three girls. But it was not the reason for the murder. If the girls had to kill their father, they would have done it right away that time.
Slowly six months passed. The girls kept on suffering silently.

It was an extreme enduring the torture. One day the three had discussed. All three had decided that now they do not have to remain silent on the atrocities of their father. If it is too much, they will leave the house and go away. They will work hard somewhere for living. If they have to live by begging, even then it will be better than this life.

One day Ehsan returned from the shop. He had brought a bottle of liquor with him. As soon as he came, he went to his room and started drinking alcohol. At that time, Ehsaan was under severe alcoholism. He called Mariam to his room-
—"Mariam, Mariam, where are you?"

Mariam asked-
—"Yes, Father."

Ehsaan called her-
—"Come over here."

When Mariam started getting up, Fatima grabbed her hand, and stopped her. Mariam looked at Fatima questioningly. Fatima shook her head in a negative gesture. The three had some discussion and the three girls together reached Ehsaan's room. Seeing the three of them together, Ehsaan was at first flustered. Then started shouting in anger-
—"I had called Mariam only. Why all of you come here?"

But today all the three girls had come with the determination that now they have to oppose the oppression.

—"Mariam is over here. Whatever it is, say it. We are standing here."
Fatima said sternly.

Ehsaan started shouting-
—"You three consider yourselves very clever. I will take out all of your arrogances."

Fatima replied-
—"What will you do? Will you kill, will you rape? Now, even if you touch us, it will not be good for you."

Ehsaan and his daughters got into a heated argument. In anger, Ehsan beat up the three girls with a stick. Angry and drunk, he murmured-
—"What do you think, you will win over me? I have sent even your mother to the hell. I will kill all three of you in the same way."

—"What?"
All three were shocked.

—"...Yes...Yes, I had strangled her to death, then hung her with the fan."

But soon Ehsaan realized that something wrong had come out of his mouth. And then he fell silent. Then, he started pretending to be unconscious due to intoxication of alcohal.

Hearing this, all three were stunned. The three girls did not sleep that night. All three kept crying throughout the night, remembering their mother. For so many years, these three were tolerating atrocities. But upon hearing about the murder of their mother, the trio started hating Ehsaan immensely.

On the evening of July 7, when 47-year-old Ehsaan called his daughters, Fatima, Mariam and Qutubunissa, and put chilli on their faces, their patience broke. During the night when he slept, the girls attacked him with knives, hammers and other items in the house, inflicting fatal wounds on his head, neck and chest.
The postmortem report stated that there were deep wounds on the body of the deceased, and the cause of

death was heavy bleeding, wounds on vital organs, especially on lungs and heart. In fact, it was because of the girls' years of oppression and horrific hatred that they killed Ehsaan in such a horrific manner.

The girls were arrested. The court sent the minors - Mariam and Qutubunisa - to a juvenile correction home. Whereas Fatima, who had become an adult then, was directed to be tried for murder and criminal conspiracy.

Later, the Human Rights Commission protested and filed an application. It was said in the application that it should be treated as a case of murder in self-defense, as the three girls had committed murder protesting the torture and sexual abuse. Then public support also started gathering in support of the girls. That application of the Human Rights Commission was accepted in the court, and the three girls were acquitted.

CHAPTER 9
TWO FOREIGN SPIES

It was a historic city. I will not tell the name of the city, you will understand for yourself. There were many old temples in that area of the city. The oldest of these, was the "World Famous Temple". True to its name, the temple was also famous in all over the world.

I am a banker. I was a newcomer to that city. In the bank, I was transferred to the world famous temple branch. This branch was in the temple campus itself. Like the temple, in the bank too, there were very much crowd of people, who withdraw and deposit money. Tourists also came there a lot.

The chief priest of the temple was involved in politics. He would bring many people of the city to the bank, sometimes to get a loan, sometimes to open an account. Many of them would have remained ineligible. But in defying the pressure of the priest, I had to struggle a lot.

One day the priest came to the bank with his disciples. When I saw him, I bowed him with folded hands. Then said-

—"Hey Babaji, why did you bother? Better, you would have called us."

He smiled-

—"Oh, where is trouble? Then the work was also very important."

We ordered tea and biscuits, which the priest denied to take. He, then asked-

—"Hey, let it all be. Just tell me, whether you will do our work or not?"

I answered-

—"please order, we are here for your service."

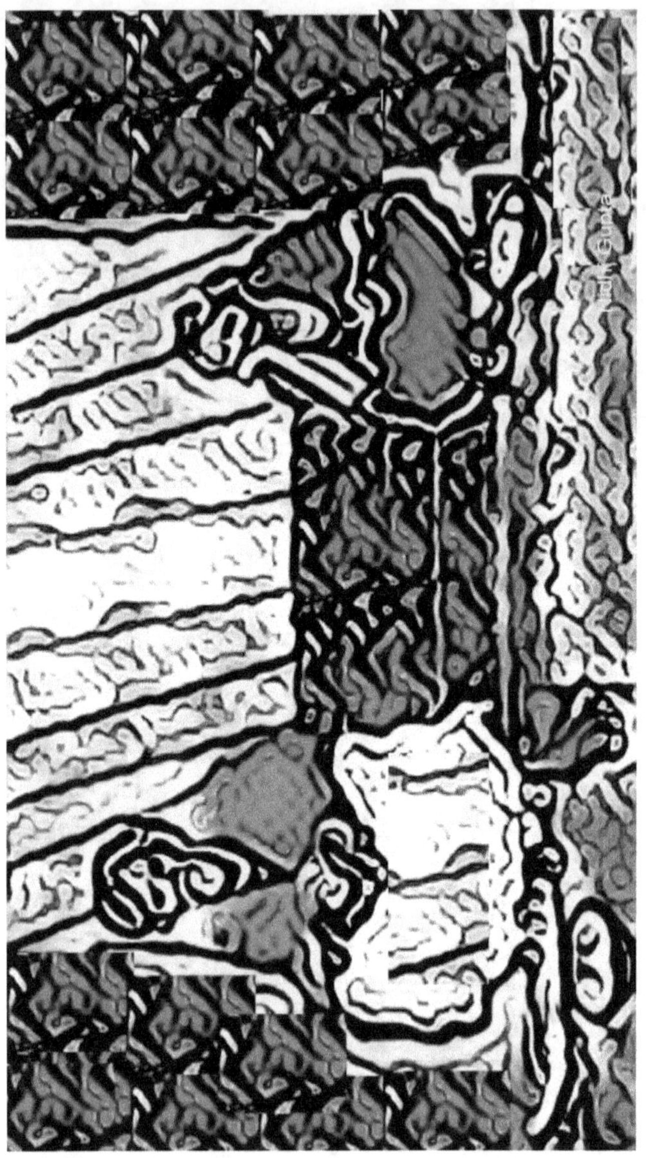

The priest started telling matter of his heart-
—"What is it that Mittal ji, the temple has a lot of land, I think that a medical college and hospital should be opened for the poors."

I was always on the lookout for a good project so that loan target of my branch could be met. I excitedly said-
—"Very good idea. You send us the project. We will finance it. We will send lawyers of the bank today itself to report on the land papers."

A week later, he sent the project worth 50 crores. Everything was going well. But when the lawyers went to see the land papers at the temple, there was a strange situation there. The lawyers knocked the door, one of the disciple of the priest opened the door.
—"We have come here to see the papers of the land."
The lawyers told his disciple.

—"You are welcome."
The disciple said, pointing the lawyers to come in.

A disciple opened the room where documents were kept. There were many big steel boxes lying there. Boxes, big and big, just like quilts, mattresses are given to daughters in dowry during weddings. The temple was spread in hundreds of acres therefore, there were too many title deeds of the land.
They were full of papers. Gnawed by rats, their feces littered with urine. Some even had termites. Lawyers would get down in those boxes by putting a ladder, then till the evening they would keep looking for the paper.
Then the lawyers shrugged off, that it is not in our capacity. However, Pujariji's mind wandered, and he postponed his plan.

Then, the government schemes came. To open an account, Jansamanya Yojana(a saving bank scheme of government for public). And for these accounts, very least KYC was prescribed as per norms. But they could not have bank balance above fifty thousand and transactions above one lakh.

Somebody spreaded a rumor that the government will put money in these accounts for free. After this, there was a flood of customers in the bank. I reach home every night at nine to ten o'clock. There was also a fear that under pressure and haste, some wrong account might be opened or the wrong person might get a loan. However, it was going on like this.

There was a Ram Janki Nagar colony behind the temple.

Outside Ram Janki Nagar Colony, an old man and an old woman used to sit and beg. No one knew where they had come from. They had also made their camp there with the help of plastic sacks. The old lady used to wear a discolored salwar kameez. The old man wore kurta pajamas. A turban of a saffron cotton cloth was tied on his head. They always took a aluminum bowl in hand in which pennies were filled. Both used to show it and beg.

A carnival was used to organized in the temple in January-February every year. A huge crowd of saints and priests gathered there. There would be a lot of food distribution and langar (free cooked meal to all people) would also run. Together, the shopkeepers put up their own shops there. Hindu Muslims all, there was no discrimination. Beggars also set up their camp during the fair. People donate with an open hand. When the carnival ends, everyone go back. Both these old couple had also come to the carnival last year. The carnival was over but they were stayed there.

The old man was probably a bit mentally unsound, and god knows what he used to murmur in himself. Sometimes, he even abuse the passers-by passing by. But the passers-by would have taken pity on him instead of anger and they would give alms. Some would give grains, some would give money. That's just what they was going through.

On the way to the bank from my house, they would occasionally meet me on the roadside at their tent. I would often run away from them in fear that the old man may attack on me, although it had never happened.

Inside the temple, the priest, using his influence, got organized a voter ID card and Aadhaar (unique identification card in India) camp. Both those two old beggars also got their voter ID card and Aadhar card made by joining the camp and after a lot of begging and persuasion.

Then, one day the list of account opening applications came from the local body of the city. The DM there called a meeting of all the bank managers of the city. DM threatened everyone in the meeting-

—"We have to say with great regret that the pace of opening of accounts is very slow in the Jansamanya Yojana (a saving bank scheme of government for public). If all the accounts are not opened in two days, then FIR will be lodged against the erring bank managers."

I vehemently requested that some of the people in the list do not have complete KYC.

DM—"Amazing you do manager. There is so much pressure from higher authority and you are clinging to KYC. You are just opening the account? Not going to give loan to them."

My senior manager Mishraji signaled me to keep quiet by pressing my hand with his. The meeting was over.

In next two-three days, due to the hard work of the bankers night and day, all the accounts were opened. Amongst them, accounts of those two beggars also had been. We have opened their accounts by taking their adhar card. A Jansamanya account has been opened of them. Only a small amount was deposited in it.

Meanwhile, one day, a guard inside the temple was murdered. Someone had killed him by slitting his throat. And hid the corpse in the bushes.
In the morning, Jairam, the cleaning worker, was sweeping there. There, he felt some strange smell. When he went ahead, he saw that the guard was lying face down. Some blood was also spread in the grass. Jairam panicked.

He shouted-
—"..murder....blood...blood...!"
Making noise, he called all the people working there.

One asked-
—"What happened? Whose blood had you seen? Where's the blood?"

Jairam pointed with a trembling finger-
—"There in the bushes."

When everyone looked in the bushes, there was a dead body. Immediately, the police was informed.

The police came to investigate. There was a lot of questioning. The priest had also reached there. The policeman asked-
—"Who saw the corpse first?"

One told-
—"Jairam. He was sweeping there. He felt some strange smell there. When he went ahead, he saw the guard's body lying in the bushes."

The police again asked-
—"Anyone seen the murderer? Has anyone come here?"

The disciple of the priest replied-
—"No."

—"Has the deceased had a quarrel or enmity with anyone?"

—"No, there was no such thing."

There was a knife lying there. There was blood on it. The knife seemed to be a simple vegetable cutter, but it had tooth like saw. It could not kill anyone, but could be used well to slit the throat.
It was told that the knife belonged to the deceased, who used to keep it with him to eat fruits etc. after chopping with it.

From this it could be inferred that either the deceased must have been sedated before being killed, or that the murderers must have been two in number. One must have held him, the other must have slit him in the throat. Otherwise, it would have been impossible to slit the throat with that knife.
The later was more likely because there were signs of struggle in the bushes. This showed that the deceased was not only conscious, but he must have fought with murderer till he died.

However, the police did a *Panchnama* (paperwork) and sent the body for post-mortem. The post-mortem report came on the next day. The cause of death given in the report was `significant jugular vein rupture and excessive bleeding.

There was an apprehension that some thief must have come to the temple to steal donation boxes or jewelery on the idols. Then when caught, he would have killed the guard and fled. But nothing was missing, neither was the sanctum sanctorum nor the lock of the donation box was broken. The nearby grass was mutilated and there were signs of struggle, whereas thieves do not fight and on such occasions often run away. The guard had only one stick to defend.
No fingerprints were found on murder weapon. Perhaps, they were cleared by the murderer.

The matter was related with the temple. There was a possibility of an outbreak of Hindu-Muslim riots. Consequently, anti riot Section 144 was imposed in the city.
But what had been feared, had happened. There was a lot of uproar in the city, and curfew was imposed. Then the case was registered in the name of unknown thieves. Later, the matter was covered up and then closed.

Then, suddenly the disease of corona had spread, and there was lockdown had been imposed. Everyone got upset. All business stopped. Migrant laborers started migrating. Some became victims of starvation.
Both those old man and old lady also stopped getting begging. If any on duty policeman there or someone else residing nearby took pity, then they would have given them something to eat. Otherwise they had to be slept hungry. They were in very bad condition.

When the effect of Corona subsided, the lockdown was relaxed. But everyone was troubled within oneself, so who would have been giving alms to those old couple?

Meanwhile, one day, a man named Amar passed by and made a sad video of the old couple and posted it on the internet. In the video, Amar asked-
—"Baba, how much do you earn here?"

The old man said helplessly-
—"Earlier, both of us old person used to eat lentils and chapati. But now for many days, we have to sleep with hungry stomach."

—"Don't you have any son or daughter?"

—"If we had any support, would we be begging here?"
Saying that the old lady started sobbing and weeping. The old man began to wipe her tears.

—"So you see, how upset these two are. If you want to help them, send money to their bank account number shown on the screen."
Amar appealed to the people.

That video went viral on the internet. From then onwards, money started coming in the accounts of the old man and the old lady.
Not only this, Amar collected a lot of money by putting video of those old beggars on some crowd funding websites and gave it to the old man.
Crowdfunding website are those websites, on which you can put an appeal for your help. The objective can be anything, such as academics, medical or political. This website takes its commission and collects small donation amounts and gives it to you.

However, a huge amount – close to 10 lakhs had been deposited. The old man was now walking stiffly. He bought dark black colored glasses from the street vendor there. He also tied an orange cloth around his neck like a scarf. People laughed at him thinking him a crazy.

One day I was sitting in the branch. Then I got a call from the head office of the my bank-
—"Hello Mittalji, Namaskar, I am speaking from the head office."

I also bade namste in reply.

—"Mittalji, do you check the daily monitoring report of your branch or not."

—"Yes, I do, but due to busy schedule I can't see all the items."

—"Then start looking by today itself. See, in your branch, ten lakh rupees have been collected in a Jansamanya account. Normally, in the Jansamanya account, there cannot be transactions of more than rupees one lakh. Balance is also more than the rule. You should freeze the account immediately."

The point was right. This was the account of those old beggar couple. I froze the account immediately.

The next day the old men and women came to our branch and approached the cashier.

—"We have to withdraw money."
Their withdrawal slip was filled by the peon. They both had marked their thumbs sign in the withdrawal slip.

Cashier said-
—"Give me the withdrawal slip."

Old man gave the withdrawal slip.
The cashier checked on her computer and said-
—"You can't get your money out. Your account is showing freeze."

—"Meaning?"
Both the old person were surprised.

—"Account freeze means... that you will not be able to withdraw money from your account."
The cashier tried to explain unsuccessfully.

—"Why can't I take out money? We have money in the account, we will withdraw whenever we want."
Both of them started shouting.

The cashier did not think it right to debate with them, and at the time many people were also standing in line waiting for their turn. She said-
—"You go and talk to the branch manager."

Both came to me and complained about account closure.

—"Our account has been closed. You took our money. Open it immediately or else I will file an FIR with the police."

We the bankers tried to explain the rules to them, but all was in vain. Those people made a lot of noise. The rest of the customers, too, were feeling more sympathy to both of them.
The next day, they also lodged an FIR against the bank. In the FIR, I and Mishraji, who was working with me,

were accused of wrongful closure of the account and money embezzlement. I was surprised that how the police, who reluctant to write the report of the common people, is showing so much speed. Later, it came to know that the priest of the temple was preparing for the election. He was helping them to get votes and to win the trust of the poor people.

The police came to the bank. There were media persons as well. I explained everything by referring to the rules. The police took the statement in writing, and went back.

I was suspecting that these old beggars were stupid in looking, from where they were getting so much brain and ideas.

The next day the news also appeared in the newspapers - the bankers misappropriated the deposits of two poor beggars.

There is a practice in a government bank, which is also mandatory by law, that any unusual transaction has to be reported to the Income Tax or various government departments. Since the account has already been frozen, our bank also reported the same.

The police and the Economic Offenses Wing launched their investigation. On getting the evidence, old man and old woman and Amar (who raised money through crowdfunding and posting videos) were arrested. The inquiry began. At first they both kept on playing. Then the in-charge of the police station asked in a stern voice-

—"You guys, tell me your real name and address. Who are you, where do you live?"

—"Hey son, those bankers ate the money of us the poors, and instead of catching them, you brought us in jail."
said the old man almost crying.

Police Incharge scolded-
—"Don't do drama here, tell the truth."

The old man again started acting of mental illness. Fell on the ground and started crying.
The old lady started cursing to the policemen-
—"Hey, you trouble we destitute poors. You will die with a death of mole."

The policemen called the mental disease doctor. He checked and told that both are completely healthy. The policemen made some plans, and told that the old man would have to be given shock treatment. Preparations were being made to give shock-treatment to the old man by holding him.
The old man got frightened, and forgot all the drama and started joining hands and feet. On strictly interrogating, they both broke up. They started answering like a parrot.

—"Tell me your real name."

The old man said-
—"Omar Sheikh, District Karachi, Pakistan."

Old lady-
—"Bilkis Bano, Sindh, Pakistan."

The police again asked-
—"The purpose of coming here?"

—"Blow up the temple with a bomb."

—"Who sent you here?"

—"Our boss."

Investigation revealed that the old man's real name was Umar Sheikh and the old woman's name was Bilkis. Both were ISI agents. Both were spying with a plan to blow up the world famous temple with a bomb. They thought that if the temple was blown up with a bomb, a Hindu Muslim riot would erupt in the city. In addition, they had also made a plan to create a riot by distributing money to the rioters in the city. On their trail, the police also recovered bomb making material from a ruined building outside the city. They had also killed the guard of the temple.

One day while they were spying in the temple, the guard saw them. Perhaps, the guard had heard some of their conversation too.

The guard shouted-

—"Who... who is there?"

Both fell silent and held their breath. They were hiding in the bushes at that time.

The guard shouted again-

—"Whoever it is, get out. Otherwise, if I come there, it will be very bad."

He said, waving his stick in the air.

Then, on not getting any answer, the guard subsided the bushes with his hands. Both appeared. But suddenly, Umar swooped down and knocked the guard down. The guard's baton swung away and fell. The guard's mouth was held by Umar with his hand so that he could not shout.

Umar was a trained spy. There was a wonderful agility in him.

Here Bilkis, groped guard's bag lying on his chair. A knife was found in it. The old lady took out the knife and slit the guard's throat. The poor guard didn't even get a chance to scream. The old man and the old lady feared that if noticed by the guard, their mission would fail and both of them killed the guard with fear of being caught.

At earlier, they had no shortage of funds. Local agent Amar was giving them money. But then due to the increase in the movement of police during the lockdown, they had to face a lot of problem.
These two had completed their spying. They also needed money to buy bomb manufacturing supplies.
Local agent, who was living in the city as Amar, planned and pretended to collect money by posting videos and crowd funding. Actually, all the money was belonging to him, which he gave to the crowdfunding website. The same money was divided into hundreds of small pieces by the crowd funding website, and put it in the old man's account.

But the problem for them was that, they got involved the bank in all this, otherwise they would have been successful in their plan. With the care of the bank, the foreign spies were busted in time and a terrorist incident in the city was avoided.
Omar Sheikh, Bilkis and Amar were handed over to the Anti-Terrorism Cell, which will further investigate that where and how much places their network is spread.

However, the Aadhar activists, who had made the Aadhar card of Omar Sheikh, Bilkis, were accused of negligence by police in court. Legal proceedings were also taken against them.

Action was not taken against the bankers. As not only did the Aadhar card exist in the form of KYC, but also the bankers had reported the information pertaining with transaction to the government department on time.

The rest of the temple priests, who was deeply involved in politics, were also questioned. But later he was released by the police. He also gave up that from now on, he will not put pressure on the bankers unnecessarily nor will he get into the affair of getting made someone's ID etc.

Rest of the DMs, under whose pressure the bulk accounts were opened, no action was taken against them, and he still keep harassing the bankers for new schemes of the government.